I0547714

ROAMIN' 'ROUND EUROPE

©2020 Jan Frazier. All rights reserved. No part of this publication may be reproduced or used in any form or by any means, graphic, electronic or mechanical, including photocopying, recording, taping, or information and retrieval systems without written permission of the publisher. This is a work of fiction. Names, characters, businesses, places, events and incidents are either the products of the author's imagination or used in a fictitious manner. Any resemblance to actual persons, living or dead, or actual events is purely coincidental.

Published by Hellgate Press

(An imprint of L&R Publishing, LLC)

Hellgate Press

PO Box 3531

Ashland, OR 97520

email: info@hellgatepress.com

Interior & Cover Design: L. Redding

ISBN: 978-1-55571-989-0

Printed and bound in the United States of America

First edition 10 9 8 7 6 5 4 3 2 1

ROAMIN' 'ROUND EUROPE

**One Professor. Nine College Students.
Three Weeks in Europe. What Could Possibly Go Wrong?**

JAN FRAZIER

Hellgate Press   Ashland, Oregon

I'd like to dedicate this book to all of the students – both high school and college – with whom I have had the honor of taking to Europe. Each of the students comes back a more mature and wiser person for having learned the traditions and having experienced the historical sights of Europe. However, I, too, grow and change as I watch the students blossom through the unmasking of Europe.

CONTENTS

Introduction...ix

Chapter 1
Our Final Days in London......1

Chapter 2
Our Last View of London......7

Chapter 3
On Our Way to the City of Light......16

Chapter 4
Our First Paris Highlights......23

Chapter 5
Where's James?......35

Chapter 6
Third Day in Paris......41

Chapter 7
Murder...Say What?......47

Chapter 8
First Day in Amsterdam......55

Chapter 9
Going Further Afield.........67

Chapter 10
Alkmaar and Zuiderzee Musuem and
Off-the-Beaten Path in Amsterdam......77

Chapter 11
Amsterdam is Anything but Boring......85

Chapter 12
Heading Back to London......93

Chapter 13
On Our Way to Canterbury...98

Chapter 14
I'll Be Roamin' 'Round Europe......104

Acknowledgments......114

About the Author......115

Works Cited......116

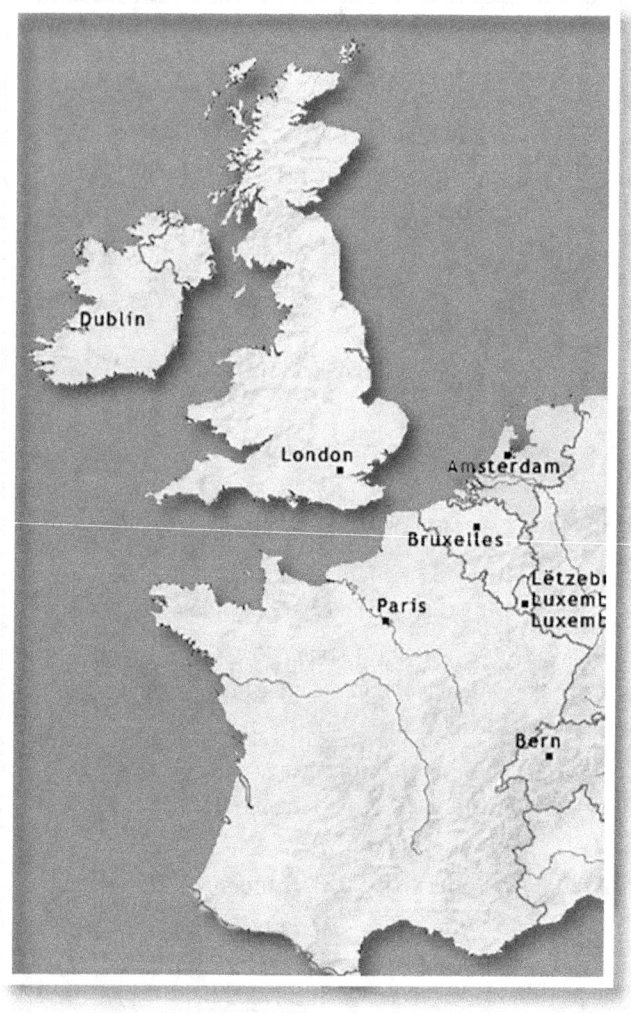

INTRODUCTION

Having been a teacher for nearly forty-five years, I looked back on many of the situations in which I found myself as I took students to Europe during the summer and during January Interim. We had some crazy times as well as some scary ones. I incorporated some of those into this novel, but then much is fictional as well.

I had always told my students that they couldn't learn everything within the four walls of the classroom; they needed to get out there in the world and see those things about which they had read. That's when everything would come to life.

I hope that you enjoy reading this book. Truly, it's about learning and growing as you delve into difficult as well as fun experiences; it's also about learning the value of travel as you mature. Have fun reading of the adventures of the study-abroad group!

CHAPTER 1

OUR FINAL DAYS
IN LONDON

I lay in bed watching the curtains billow in the morning breeze, and the east window allowed slanted golden sun rays to fall across the floor. *It must be after 6:00 a.m.*, I thought. My watch said 6:15.

I pulled myself from bed and walked to the window to inhale the golden air. The breeze carried with it the sound of music playing at the small outdoor café near the hotel. It was a catchy tune and sounded vaguely familiar. American music was not uncommon in England. Finally, I flopped back down on my bed and closed my eyes, reliving a few moments of the incredible theater production we had seen the previous night.

Shakespeare's *Macbeth* was the reason I hadn't gotten back to the hotel until 11:00 p.m. and finally to sleep around midnight. Even though it was only 6:15, I knew I needed to rise and finish grading papers before breakfast and then class. I had suggested that we start class a bit later – 9:00 instead of 8:00 – since it had been a late night at the theater.

It was my fifth year of taking college students to Europe during the May-Interim for a three-week study abroad course, resulting in four hours of credit at our university. When my husband passed away six years ago, I decided to teach the May-Interim because I loved to travel. With his illness, we hadn't been able to go places, and I had really missed that opportunity. I loved watching the students view Europe for a first time and actually experience what they had read. It was my firm belief that a teacher could only teach so much within the four walls of a classroom, and then the students had to get out there and actually experience the places about which they had read.

On this trip, we started in London, would move to Paris, and then to Amsterdam. We'd take the ferry back to London to spend one last day before flying back to the States. Actually, I would be staying in Europe after the students left to visit friends in Holland – I had previously lived in The Netherlands for several years – and then going to Munich to see my German relatives.

We had quite a time getting to London because of an electrical storm over Chicago. We sat for seven hours on the runway before our flight left, and then we had to land in Iceland for half of the night because of another storm. In all, we missed a full day in London, and I felt so bad for the students – who seemed to take it in stride.

It was now our fifth day in London with one day left before we caught the train to the mainland via the Chunnel.

"Need coffee," I muttered to myself as I made my way to the electric coffee pot that the hotel had provided just for people like me who couldn't make it until breakfast to get her fix of caffeine. For this reason alone, I had chosen this hotel. Well, not really. I wanted the students to experience something that wasn't American and modern – no contemporary, avant-garde hotel that could accommodate hundreds of people in their large, elaborately decorated rooms. St. Giles Hotel was typically European – rich in culture, traditionally old but well-kept with a very small-cubical-sized elevator – in the middle of a narrow, busy street bustling with traffic and all drivers blaring their horns on their way to work. It was typically old-world European at its best.

Being a professor of English and teaching "Study Abroad Travel Writing" to the nine students enrolled in my class, I was continually grading journals and essays that were required for the course. I still had three essays to finish before I got to breakfast at 8:00 and to class by 9:00.

We had visited the Tower of London, Windsor Castle, Piccadilly Circus, Westminster Abby, Big Ben, the British Museum, and so much more. After class today, we'd start by traveling to Buckingham Palace to see the Changing of the Guard and then make our way to St. Paul's Cathedral to end our day.

I spent the next hour and a half grading the essays. In the thirty years in which I had been teaching English, I felt that I had literally lugged essays along wherever I went, hoping to have a moment to further my grading – to the hairdresser, nail tech, my children's dance classes, and sometimes even to my school functions. I bitterly envied the math teachers who left school with no papers at all to grade.

By 7:45 I was done, and I quickly applied a little make-up and ran a comb through my short blonde hair. My natural curl made this cut simple to comb and style, and I smiled that it only took minutes to be ready. My clothes were laid out for the day, and as I slipped into them, I smiled as I thought that it took me less time than my son to get ready in the morning.

Breakfast was simple – a buffet of buttered toast, hard-boiled eggs, various meats, an assortment of fruit, and coffee or tea. I waved at a group of my students at a nearby table as I took a seat in the corner and caught up on a few emails as I ate.

Class started at 9:00 in the conference room of the hotel. It was a nice room with a long table – nothing fancy but clean and well equipped for meetings with a chalk board, flip chart, and an overhead projector.

"Well, good morning, class," I said, attempting always to be upbeat and chipper no matter how tired I may have been. "How did you enjoy *Macbeth* last night?" I questioned as I made my way to the end of the table.

"Awesome."

"It was extraordinary."

"Long," I heard from the other end of the table. "Don't get me wrong. It was good. I just needed some sleep," groaned James.

I smiled and nodded. "Let's start with reading aloud from our journals concerning yesterday's Tower of London excursion and then our thoughts on last night's play."

Our class period continued with journal readings, a short grammar lesson, and finally the topic of this day's activities.

Rodney raised his hand. "I have a question, Professor Kira."

Carolyn had asked one day in class if they could use my first name, and a nod of the head and a grin from me confirmed the idea.

"What is it, Rod?"

"Why don't the Londoners smile? I mean, they all look like someone just died and they're going to a funeral."

The class snickered but agreed.

"You know," I replied, "I've been asked that question about Europeans before. My only response is that Americans are just more friendly and smile more. We don't think about that because it's normal to us."

"Well, I'm setting a goal for today," continued Rodney. "I'm going to try to get the Londoners on the Tube to smile."

"Me, too," chimed in James.

"Okay," I acknowledged with a grin. "Let us know in class tomorrow of your results. By the way, we'll have class tomorrow after our Chunnel ride to Paris. However, I'm dismissing class a little early today so that we get to Buckingham Palace on time to see the Changing of the Guard, which takes place at 11:00. Katie, you and Lisa are in charge of getting us there today so plan the route," I concluded.

The first night we had arrived in London, I had explained the subway system in detail, including the use of the buses. By buying their week-long passes in advance – which would have been overwhelming to them all in itself – I had saved time on our first city. After going through the transportation details, I took them to Big Ben via the Tube and told them they now had to find their way back to the hotel on their own.

"What!" Jessa exclaimed. "Alone?"

Everyone looked at me, wide eyed and a bit taken-aback, awaiting my answer.

"Not alone. Stay in pairs or a small group. You can do this," I commented with confidence. "I'll see you at breakfast tomorrow morning," I concluded to the still-astonished young people. However, in a few seconds, they had turned their attention to their underground maps and had started planning their return trip.

I had told the students before we left the States that they'd come home different people, and they had laughed. After being in Europe less than a week, they already understood my remark. New sights, different cultures, and rich, old traditions had opened their eyes to a glimpse of a world they hadn't anticipated. Soon they would have an even bigger eye-opener – we'd be heading into a world that didn't speak English as a first language.

CHAPTER 2

OUR LAST VIEW OF LONDON

I t was 9:45 and all the students disappeared to their rooms to retrieve their jackets – it was May but still a bit chilly – and dispense with everything except small notebooks for the next day's journal entries.

Katie and Lisa gave their nonessential items to their roommates to take to their rooms so they could work out the strategic plan to get to Buckingham Palace. Our hotel – St. Giles – was across from Russell Square, so the Tube stop was literally our next-door neighbor.

By the time everyone had returned, the girls were ready with our mapped-out route. By now, I trusted the students' judgment on how to get to a particular place. In the beginning, I checked their route to make any shortcuts, but they were now as good as I was at planning the Tube route.

Hustling to the Tube, we made short work of the few stops that we had to make to get to Buckingham, arriving there by 10:50. Getting out of the subway stop was the most difficult because so many others were trying to make their way to the Changing of the Guard.

"You'll love this ceremony," I commented as we walked toward the crowded mass in front of Buckingham. "This daily event is such a regal display because it is the official transfer of the Palace's military security. It possesses the same formality that it did centuries before. Amazing, I think, because Europe thrives on their rich, old traditions, and so often, we in America replace our heritage and culture with something new and modern."

As soon as we had squeezed into the crowd, we could begin to hear the sound of trumpets and drums.

"It's straight up 11:00, so they are right on time. Can everyone see?"

"I can't see very well," Carolyn shouted.

"Here, get in front of me," I signaled as she wiggled her way through the massive crowd.

There was something about those splendid red uniforms, the tall black hats, and the precision of dozens of soldiers marching majestically to their music that would send chills up my spine every time that I would see it.

As the soldiers made their way in front of us, Carolyn commented to me, "It's breathtaking because they are so perfect in marching, playing their instruments, and rotating and spinning their rifles that I'm mesmerized by the entire procession. I can't imagine the hours of practice they have put into being so accomplished."

CHANGING OF THE GUARD

"Yes, they are amazing," I inserted. "Another Changing of the Guard is happening right now at Windsor Castle. It's a smaller version but just as precise and beautiful."

Rodney called over his shoulder, "I want to come back tomorrow to see this again."

"Impossible. We'll be on our way to Paris at this time tomorrow."

He laughed. "I know but nothing can be as amazing as this."

"Oh, my dear young man, you just wait and see. You're going to be in the "City of Light," and you'll have to eat your words, I'm afraid. However, remember that we're returning to London to catch our flight back to the States. We'll have a day to experience Canterbury, where Chaucer's *Canterbury Tales* took place. It's a city with a cathedral like no other that you'll see."

* * * *

By mid-afternoon, we found ourselves at St. Paul's Cathedral.

"You did a great job today, Lisa and Katie, getting us to our destinations. Good work!"

Lisa bowed and Katie curtsied as if acknowledging a member of the royal family.

"Dismissed now," I said with a feigned royal command.

I heard snickers from the others as we continued.

The magnificence of the cathedral started right at the steps with the giant pillars. I attempted to give them background information about the cathedral before we actually entered through the West Porch entrance.

"Christopher Wren rebuilt this cathedral after the Great Fire of London in 1666. The fire left the structure in ruins as it did many other buildings in the city. Wren had an even grander plan in mind, but because of finances, he had to 'water down' his plan. I'll tell you more once we're inside."

We entered through the massive doors to the grandeur of the cool, extremely spacious interior. It was perfectly quiet inside – almost eerily still – as most people normally stood in awe during their entire visit at the cathedral.

DOME OF ST. PAUL'S CATHEDRAL

Lisa turned to me and whispered, "This is 'watered down'? Whoa!"

I smiled and nodded.

The interior of the cathedral integrated the grandeur of great classical churches with Baroque sculptures, and its giant gilded piers artfully disguised the supporting structures. An enormous, awe-inspiring church, St. Paul's sported huge, domed arches, all finished in gilded frescoes and fantastic, colorful mosaics.

I motioned for the students to sit in the pews part way up the aisle so we could see all of the Baroque splendor from a closer angle.

"Some of the most elaborate celebrations have taken place here. The funeral of Winston Churchill and the wedding of Prince Charles and Lady Diana to name a few."

No one had spoken anything since Lisa's comment, and I finally continued. "I want you to look straight up at the dome." No one had even seen the dome yet as they were focused on the grandiose sights in front of them. "From the outside, the dome is 360 feet high, which makes it the second biggest dome in the world. Only St. Peter's in Rome surpasses it. Unbelievably, the huge, gilded dome weighs 84,000 tons. The railing that you see encloses the area called the Whispering Gallery. We're going to climb the 259 steps that will take us up there. It's called the Whispering Gallery because you can stand on one side of the dome and whisper, and the person on the opposite side can hear. It's amazing!"

Still no one had said a word but only stared at

WHISPERING GALLERY, ST. PAUL'S

the beauty and magnificence of Wren's incredible masterpiece.

We spent the next hour climbing the stairs and whispering in the Gallery – of course, everyone had to have a chance at whispering. Another 330 steps would have taken us to the top of the dome, creating a bird's eye view of London. However, we decided to call it a day and returned to the Tube station. We had a favorite café near our hotel where we found ourselves at 6:00.

We allowed ourselves the luxury of pushing tables together so that we could review the day's activities.

"I saw all of you taking copious notes today during our Tube ride after the Changing of the Guard and when sitting in St. Paul's. You should have some incredible journal entries tomorrow. You'll have time to write during our Chunnel ride to Paris. It'll take two hours," I concluded.

"I think that you saved the best for last," commented Sara, who was the quiet one of the nine students. "St. Paul's was totally beyond comprehension."

"I did want you to have a final lasting memory of London. I was here in London a few years ago at Thanksgiving. Of course, Londoners don't celebrate our Thanksgiving, but, remarkably, St. Paul's holds a Thanksgiving service for any Americans in London. I can't begin to tell you the magnificence of the choir as they sang that day. It was all more than spectacular," I stated. "But we'll return here for our flight back home, and our quick trip to Canterbury will be excellent before leaving Europe for good.

"By the way, Rodney, did you succeed in getting anyone to smile? Wasn't that your goal today?"

His sheepish grin told me he hadn't.

"No, but I tried. Are the French the same way? I have a week to get them to smile," Rod continued.

"You may find that they are a little easier, but, remember, most Europeans don't smile to strangers. They are fine in a group of people whom they know. Keep trying. It's a really good goal," I responded.

I packed that night to ready myself for our trip to Paris, but I had to bet that many of the students went out to celebrate the memories they had gathered in the grand city of London and left the packing until morning. At any rate, all of us boarded the 10:00 a.m. train that would take us under the English Channel to the "City of Light" and to alarming – no, horrifying – circumstances that we weren't expecting.

CHAPTER 3

ON OUR WAY TO "THE CITY OF LIGHT"

Even though it was a two-hour trip, it seemed much shorter. We traveled through the green English countryside with picturesque country houses and red and blue flowers dotting the hillsides until we arrived at the English Channel. Once there, we entered the tunnel which would take us across to France.

It was like any other tunnel through the Alps in Italy or Switzerland, only this tunnel was underwater – the English Channel. Thus, the name "Chunnel" was derived. There wasn't a lot to see during the long tunnel ride, so the students spent their time writing notes about the trip so far and putting last-minute remarks in their journals, which would be due when we arrived in Paris.

I could tell from the bits and pieces that I picked up from the conversations that most of the students had gone out for a drink or two the night before. Drinking was legal in Europe, and all of these students were of age – according to European standards – and their only rule was that they needed to be in class – and on time – the next day. Oh, yes, and alert. So far, everything had run smoothly.

As we exited the tunnel and arrived in France, we found ourselves surrounded by lush green vineyards with small villages dotting the countryside. Steeples in every town pointed skyward. The noon sky was noticeably brighter, but with the sprinkling of clouds, long shadows erupted from the villages. Even the vineyards seemed to have a golden haze cast on them, and workers waved as we passed in the train.

"I like these French people already," said Rodney. "They may not smile on the subway – I don't know that yet – but they wave from the vineyards!"

That got a snicker from everyone.

"You know," continued Rodney, "I want to see more of Europe. Just this small taste has only whetted my appetite for more."

"Same here," chimed in James. "Italy is next on my list."

"I can understand that," I inserted. "With a surname like Giovanni, why not?"

James smiled. "I'll have to tell you my story because I'm really going to Italy next. My grandfather came from a small village in Sicily, and my brother showed me an interesting article in the newspaper a few weeks ago. There are some rural villages in Sicily – my grandfather's village for one – who have lost many people to large cities north of Sicily, and many houses there were left empty. The government is trying to bring life back into these less-occupied places in these villages that are steeped in rich history.

"Guess how much the houses are selling for," commented James.

"I don't know, but I'm betting pretty cheap if there isn't much business in the villages," answered Rita.

"One Euro!" exclaimed James. "Can you imagine that? That's a dollar and a little change in American money. I guess that it has been all over the social media, and the rural villages are now luring new residents by offering these centuries-old homes for sale for one Euro. Americans, Canadians, and Swiss are buying the structures and getting the villages back on their feet. Some of these places are becoming resorts, hotels, casinos, waterparks, condominiums, and others are simply being made into family homes. However, these foreigners who are buying the homes are also creating businesses in the villages – restaurants, hardware stores, grocery stores, and even schools.

"My brother, who is an architect, is in the process of buying an old, vacant house in Cantiano, which is a rural area of Sicily where Grandpa was born. Since I'm in electrical engineering at school, he has offered to take me along in June to help him. He has already been told that there is no electricity or running water in the house. It's definitely a fixer-upper," concluded James with a wide grin.

"That is the most exciting thing that I've heard in a long time," I said, smiling at his luck. "You'll have to keep us informed, James."

He nodded.

The rest of the class continued to chat with James about the amazing prospect while I sat back and gazed ahead, hoping to get a glimpse of the metropolis that would soon be upon us. Yes, Paris.

"Ten extra credit points for the first person to see the top of the Eiffel Tower," I shouted for everyone to hear.

Within the next ten minutes, Sara and Jessa both shouted at the same time that they had a glimpse of the Eiffel, and I made a note to add points to the two girls' grades.

I pulled from a memory of the past: "I remember some years ago, a friend and I were driving to Paris – well, not exactly Paris but rather to Versailles, which is the grand palace south of Paris. We were staying in a hotel near Versailles, and I especially wanted to miss Paris."

"How so? I'd have thought that you'd want to see Paris," questioned Brad, who was another quiet one like Sara.

"Yes, I wanted to *see* Paris, not drive *through* it. That was precisely why we were not staying in the center of the city. Anyway, as I started the sentence, 'If you see the Eiffel Tower, we're in trouble because....'"

"I think you're too late," interrupted my friend, Karen. "There it is, Kira."

I heard a mutual giggle from the students.

"What did you do then?" asked Carolyn.

"I pulled into the first gas station that I could find. I must have looked lost with my map – fully opened –

and my glasses perched on my nose, trying to sort out where the heck we were. Two or three nice French gentlemen asked – in English, I might add – where I was trying to go. I told them Versailles, and they attempted to map out the route for me. Finally, one of the nice fellows said, 'Follow me. I'm going to take you most of the way. When I turn off, you continue on until you see the sign that says Versailles. It will be simple, yes?'"

"I have to say that I was amazed at the kindness. The French have a reputation of being a little standoffish sometimes, but these were real gentlemen."

As we slowly rolled into the terminal, I knew that I had to change the subject and approach a topic that was important for the students to know.

"Now, I want to tell you something – not to scare you but to warn you. There are pickpockets everywhere in Paris, especially at the train station, so watch your possessions carefully. Don't be sidetracked by people bumping into you or children coming up to you to beg. Chances are, they are a distraction, drawing your attention to them so the pickpocket can do his thing.

"And another thought – watch out for each other. For example, Sara, you might see something happening to Katie that she doesn't notice. Stay two or three together at all times."

Everyone was looking at each other with a sense of defensiveness that they hadn't had or needed in London.

Slowly the train was coming closer to the end of the track.

We'll be coming into the Gare du Nord – North Station – so have a look at your maps that I gave you and find that station. We're going to take the Metro to our hotel, which is near the Champs Elysees and the Arc de Triomphe. Once we're on the Metro it shouldn't take too long...."

I never finished my sentence because out of the corner of my eye, I had a glimpse of flashing lights – actually, a string of lights all atop police cars. And it wasn't just the police cars that caught my attention but the gendarmes who were lined up near the station, all with rifles!

"What's happening!" exclaimed James. "Professor Kira, what do you think?"

"Only one thing would bring all of the police out like this – an act of terror."

Just then the conductor came onto the P.A. system, announcing something in French. My French wasn't the best because of the lack of use, but I could pick up enough to know that I had been right.

"All right, class, we hang very close together. There have been several acts of terror in Paris last night. I've been in Paris after a terrorist attack, and if the terrorist has moved on – and he probably has if he hasn't made another move since last night – then right here is the safest place you can be. Everything is secure because the gendarmes are on high alert. No one can make a move without someone on the force seeing it. We needn't be afraid."

I believed what I said, but still I was feeling a little skeptical myself. What if the terrorist hadn't left and was waiting for another chance to attack? I believed what I told the students, but still a part of me went rigid.

The train came to a stop inside of the terminal, and people were mumbling to each other, but there was no panic. The passengers picked up their bags and awaited the door of the train to open. Already I could see armed gendarmes outside of the train – all on alert.

"I want all of you to follow me. Stay in twos, and don't get out of line or fall behind. James, I want you to bring up the rear. I'm going to head for the Metro, and we'll have three or four stops before we get off. We don't have to switch trains so that's good. The Metro is another place that is a pickpocket haven, so watch out for each other."

As I suspected, the Metro was packed, but the atmosphere was one of quiet alert. Acts of terrorism were not new to the Parisians, and they knew that it was as safe as possible with their excellent system of protection from the gendarmes.

Our hotel was on a tiny side street located directly behind the beautiful boulevard of Champs Elysees. Even though it was just a short walk from our Metro stop to the hotel, I felt a certain guarded feeling in my gut. We all hung together, and within fifteen minutes, we were at the hotel.

I opened Hotel MacMahon's door, and the students entered. Even with all of the encouragement that I had given the students, I let out an audible sigh of relief when we were finally in the lobby.

CHAPTER 4

OUR FIRST PARIS HIGHLIGHTS

The checking-in process was always a bit hectic, and because the MacMahon Hotel had a very small lobby, most of the students tried to find a seat or stood looking out the window. Putting my thoughts of terrorism aside for the time being, I inhaled the scent of fresh gardenias. I was always amazed at the Europeans' love of beautiful flowers, which were displayed in every hotel, banquet hall, and restaurant.

I waited patiently for my turn to register the students. It's never a quick process. Finally, it was my turn, but then the red tape seemed to go on forever – students' names, passport numbers, home addresses, and cell phone numbers. I never understood the super-efficiency of the French at the hotels. Eventually I was given the keys. I called the students two by two and handed them two large keys.

"As you can see, the keys are large. Girls, put them into an inner pocket of your purse, and, guys, put them in your front pocket.

"Oh, and maybe you've already noticed that the elevator is extremely small. My suggestion is to put your luggage on the elevator, push the button for your floor, and then you climb the stairs. One of you go up first and be ready for the luggage."

"Well, this should be interesting," piped in Carolyn. "Something new for us," she said with a laugh. "It looks like a closet."

I grinned. "Feel lucky to have an elevator in France because many hotels don't. I've climbed to the fifth floor while towing my luggage. Remember, it's all part of our European adventure. We'll meet in that room over there," I said, pointing to an open door, "in half an hour for class. Bring your Metro maps, city maps, your journals, and questions. I'm sure you have many," I concluded with a smile.

I felt relieved that we had class now because I wasn't certain about going out on the streets. I talked with the concierge, and he said that he felt it was a safe call to go sightseeing.

"Of course, you can't be certain about terrorists," the concierge commented, "but the pattern has been that once they strike, they leave, hoping not to be tracked. However, the gendarmes are hot on the trail – as you Americans say – of a group that they think were involved," concluded the concierge.

Our class period was an interesting one with dozens of questions concerning the terrorists – which I didn't feel qualified to answer – and we agreed that it made for interesting journal material for the next day's writings.

For the afternoon, I decided that it best if we went to the Arc de Triomphe, which was very close, and then shop on the Champs Elysees. It was a beautiful boulevard in the daytime but exquisite at night with the streetlights brightly illuminating the buildings and the Arc. We had dinner that night at an outdoor café on the Champs Elysees and spent an hour sitting, gazing at the crowds, and soaking up the atmosphere that only Paris can generate.

As we returned to the MacMahon Hotel, the illumination from the streetlights was left behind, and the dark, tiny cobblestone street of the hotel allowed the sky to boast a moon in all its vast, ripe fullness. We all stood and looked, trying to absorb the beauty as the moon hoisted itself higher into the night sky.

"Another good topic for your journals, class. Help someone who is not standing here with us visualize this grandeur," I commented.

"I don't have words for it," whispered Carolyn. "But I'm going to try when I write my journal," she inserted with a smile.

* * * *

With no more current mishaps from the terrorists, I felt fairly safe to go "out on the town" the next day. The last item that I covered in class was the Metro and how to read the map. It was altogether different from the Tube, and once they were all totally confused, I said, "Let's start off, and I'll teach you as we go."

We set our sights on the Eiffel Tower, and then we'd end in the late afternoon and evening at Mont-

ARC DE TRIOMPHE

martre, which is the artists' paradise. In the lobby, we all took a seat on the sofas, and I gave them some facts about the Eiffel Tower. Copiously, they took notes.

"As you probably know, the Eiffel Tower wasn't meant to be a permanent structure in Paris. It was erected specifically for the World's Fair of 1889 and was to be torn down a few years later. Meanwhile, the telegraph was invented, and a wireless tower was necessary. With the Eiffel Tower being the highest structure in the world at the time, it was the perfect signaling station for the telegraph.

"Architects hated the Eiffel and called it a 'damned lamp post that ruined the skyline,' but by 1910, the lamp post was here to stay," I concluded with a grin.

"I read that there are different levels that you can stop on. May we go up or not?" asked Brad, anxiously.

"Yes, we're actually going all the way to the top. You paid for this opportunity with the fees that you paid for this class," I responded. "And, as you can imagine, the view is spectacular. Well, it you have no more questions, let's get going."

We spent three hours at the Eiffel Tower. While still on the ground, we got pictures from every angle, and we even allotted ourselves some time to lie in the grass and people watch.

"You know what I noticed," commented Rita, another one of the more quiet students, "is that people who seem to be real Parisians dress well. I mean, you don't see anyone in jogging pants or sweats. The women have dresses or nice pants with heels, and the men all look as if they are going to an office job. I mean, in the States, you see all kinds of clothes, but mostly people aren't dressed up unless they are going to work, and even then, some dress sloppily."

I laughed. "Funny you should notice that. It's true that Parisians dress well when they go out of the house. They wouldn't be caught dead in sweats, pajama pants, joggers, or anything else that is worn strictly in the house. This may sound strange, but they believe that they are 'insulting others' if they don't dress well."

"If only Americans would see it that way," responded Katie. "I hate it when people look like slobs. And if you want to see the worst dressed people of all, just go to Walmart!"

That got a laugh from the class.

Our journey to the top of the Eiffel was amazing – breathtaking is probably an even better word – as we were immersed in the beauty of Paris from the sky. Discovering a snack bar on the top floor, we found tables and chairs in one corner. Quickly, we located the Champs Elysees and the Arc de Triomphe.

As the sun sleepily made its way toward the west, I thought that perhaps we should descend and catch the Metro to the Montmartre area. However, it was difficult for me to leave the spectacle of Paris from on high. Even though I had been at the top of the Eiffel many times, I was always struck by the heart-stopping beauty of Paris. One would think that the shock would wear off and that seeing the spectacular

EIFFEL TOWER

sight would lose its power. But every time I returned to the top was like the first. I sat captivated until I knew that we had to leave in order to have time at Montmartre.

* * * *

When we got to the Metro, I stood by the map and traced our route so that the students would get the idea because tomorrow, it would be two students' job to plan our way. We got to Anvers Metro stop and exited the subway to walk the tiny, cobblestone alleys of Montmartre, heading upward to the Butte Montmartre, which still preserved the atmosphere of prewar Paris.

There was a funicular—a small, silvery cable car – that would take the crowds up the steep, grassy hillside to the Butte and Place du Tertre. However, there were also 157 steps that were far more exciting to attempt. Whole French families came out sometimes in the evenings to experience the festive atmosphere of Place du Tertre. It is there that bands play, and artists draw amazing portraits of the local crowds and tourists.

Place du Tertre looked almost like a real village with a square in the center for the artists. All around the square ran terrace restaurants with dance floors, colored lights, and people enjoying the fun. We planned a meeting place in front of a popular souvenir shop, and the students split up, many heading toward the artists to have a portrait drawn.

By the time we met up, it was becoming dusk, and

ALLEYS OF MONTMARTRE

we still hadn't been to the Sacre Coeur, the incredible white basilica, which sat on a hill of Montmartre and overlooked the whole of Paris. Lovingly called "The White Dove of Paris," the church was built on the top of a picturesque ascension of steps that allowed tourists a place to sit and absorb the beauty of Paris from afar.

"Here's a little background on Sacre Coeur," I commented as the students all sat on the steps to immerse themselves in the ambiance of Paris. "This gorgeous church was built in the late 1800s after the Franco-Prussian War. Catholic businessmen promised to build a magnificent church if God would spare France in the war. Sacre Coeur was the fulfillment of that vow."

"It's a magnificent basilica," said Carolyn, "but this panorama in front of us is indescribable."

"You are so right, Carolyn. Soak it up," I whispered.

With darkness coming quickly to the Butte Montmartre, the lights of the city had already flickered on. Every monument was alit with a flood of light, and the Seine River curled through the center of Paris as a snake-like, silvery, mesmerizing force. Most beautiful, though, was the Eiffel Tower, which pierced the dusky night as a pinnacle with hundreds of white illuminators.

We sat for ten minutes, all spellbound by the incredible display of beauty, and slowly each student took out his notebook to record impressions of the spectacle in front of us.

"I want to 'see' and 'feel' this picturesque scene tomorrow in your journals," I commented. I didn't even

LE SACRE COEUR

get a nod from anyone as they scribbled their inner-most feelings on paper.

We decided to eat at a nearby café in order to continue consuming the beauty of the "City of Light" for the next two hours. The Europeans never rush their meals, and we were glad to sit, chat, people-watch, and absorb the splendor of Paris at night.

It was 9:00 before we headed back to MacMahon Hotel, but little did we know that our evening wasn't finished yet. It would be the early hours of the morning before we got to bed.

CHAPTER 5

WHERE'S JAMES?

Instead of going straight to the Metro stop, we returned to Place du Tertre to shop at the incredible souvenir shop that we had seen. Having been there in the past, I knew that they had great Paris t-shirts, and many of the students wanted one.

It was nearly 9:30 when we arrived at Anvers Metro stop and waited to board the Metro toward Champs Elysees.

"Is everyone here?" I asked. "Let's count off."

Before we left the States, each student had a number assigned to him so that we could count off quickly in order to account for everyone.

"One," said Sara; "Two," chimed in Brad....there was silence then.

"Who is number three?" I asked.

"That's James," answered Brad.

"Where is he?" I asked, anxiously.

No one knew. Mentally, we retraced our evening and knew that he had been at dinner with us. No one seemed positive if he had been at the souvenir shop or not. Did we leave him at Place du Tertre at the souvenir shop or had he disappeared before then? I felt panic stirring in my stomach as I silently reproached myself for not having counted off before we left Montmartre.

"I don't want anyone going anywhere alone so let's all go back to Place du Tertre and see if we can find him."

I did a once-over in the souvenir shop, but there was no James. We decided to split up to search the artists' area and look in the cafes. Meeting back in ten minutes, no one had anything to report. Now what?

Remembering that James had commented after the *Macbeth* play that it was long and that he had been sleepy, I suggested that we all go back to the hotel to see if he had gone on alone to get to bed early.

The conversation on the Metro consisted of one topic – James. If he wasn't at the hotel, what were our possibilities? Kidnapping? Lost on the way to Anvers Metro stop? There weren't many ideas.

I tried to think positively that he was in bed in his room, but he wasn't.

"What should we do?" asked Rodney. "Should we split up and go look for him?"

"No, definitely I don't want you students out searching. I've lost one person – I don't want to lose one or two more." I pondered the problem. "Here's what we're going to do. All of you – except the boys and me – are going to sit in the lobby and wait. I want you to promise me that you won't go out."

They all nodded.

"Okay, the boys and I are heading back and retracing any areas that we think James may have gone. You're my safeguards, guys, so we must stay together."

"No problem," Rodney answered. "We're here to protect you, Professor Kira."

"Well, let's just hope that none of us needs protecting."

I swear that we searched every dark alleyway and winding narrow street that existed between MacMahon Hotel and Montmartre. We looked in pubs, cafes, and souvenir shops that were still open but to no avail. We were gone for over three hours and entered the hotel at 2:00 a.m. Everyone was still in the lobby – either they were slung out on the sofas or chairs asleep or chatting endlessly to each other. Their disheartened faces became more depressed when they saw that we didn't have James.

"Nothing," I commented in a dejected tone. "We've searched everywhere. Just no James."

"What now?" asked Katie and Rita, simultaneously.

"Well, there's no hotel concierge on duty, and I don't really know how to contact the police. There is an emergency number to call, but I don't know what it is. We'll have to wait until someone assumes duty at the hotel desk in the morning in order to call the gendarmes," I answered. "For now, I think that we just need to get to our rooms. If he surfaces, Rod, you need to let me know, and I'll place a phone call to each of you so you can quit worrying."

Just as I finished my remark, I looked up and saw James entering the door.

"James!" everyone exclaimed. Suddenly every dispirited student was now alive and bright eyed. Questions of "Where have you been?" "Are you okay?" "Are you hurt?" "Did someone kidnap you?"

James was silent as he pushed his way to the closest sofa and collapsed. He looked disheveled and exhausted – his shirt dirty and torn, a cut on his face, and an eye that was turning black and blue.

"I need some water," gasped James as he tried to collect himself to answer our questions. Brad went for water as we all sat waiting.

After downing a glass of water, James looked at me and said, "I'm so sorry, Professor Kira. This was a nightmare for all of you."

"We're just glad that you're here and okay. Tell us what happened," I said as I sat next to him on the sofa with my arm around him.

"I was a fool, first of all. I was so sleepy and tired after we ate that I decided to come on back to the hotel and go to sleep. All of you were in the souvenir shop, and I thought that no one would miss me. I was stupid.

"I thought that I could easily find the Metro stop, but I had forgotten its name, and, on top of that, I got lost just trying to find it. I finally ended up at the Pigalle Metro stop."

"Oh, no, James. Brothels," I remarked.

"Yes, you don't need to tell me. Prostitutes on every corner and the center of gangs or groups equivalent to gangs. I saw the Metro sign but decided it wasn't safe to try to get to it, and I turned around, but, truthfully, I had no idea which way to go to get out of that district. Anyway, by then a few of the roughnecks had seen me and ran after me. I want to tell you that I was petrified." James paused and turned to Brad. "Could you get me another glass of water, please?"

Rita pulled out a candy bar and handed it to James. He nodded his thanks.

After his second glass of water and a few bites of candy, he seemed a bit renewed and continued.

"They rattled off something in French, and I assumed they wanted money. I had only a few Euros on me and gave them that, but they weren't satisfied. They wanted more. Well, as you can see, they roughed me up to see if I was hiding anything, and finally when they realized that I had nothing, they pushed me to the ground and punched me in the eye." James hesitated a moment and then added, "But they got the key to my hotel room."

I tried to hide my astonishment, but I'm not good at covering my emotions, and I'm sure that they showed. "Oh, James, we'll work that out. Don't worry. The name of the hotel isn't on our keys, is it?"

I pulled my key out of my purse to check. MacMahon Hotel was etched in small letters on one side. I felt a surge of bile rise in my chest.

"Well, anything valuable I want you to put into my room. James, you and Rodney go to Brad's room."

"Yes, I have two double beds, and I'm the only one in the room. It'll be perfect," commented Brad.

"We'll have to wait until morning to report this to the police. Can you describe them, James?"

"Yes, I think so. It was dark but I got a pretty good look at one of them. He had a patch over his eye. He had long dark hair and a scruffy-looking beard."

"Well, here's the good point," I commented. "Someone like that wouldn't come around the MacMahon Hotel because he just wouldn't fit into this area."

"No, but he could send one of the prostitutes. She could dress so that she would be unnoticed," concluded James.

Yes, I thought silently. *He has a point.* However, I kept that to myself.

"We had better all say a prayer of thanks tonight for James' safe return," I said as I checked my watch. "It's now 3:00, so let's all hit the hay. We're going to wait until noon to have our class – which cuts into our sightseeing time – but all of us need the sleep."

I gave James a big hug.

"There's an ice machine on your floor, James, and there's a bucket for the ice and a plastic bag inside of it. Rodney, could you get ice for James to put on that eye? Let's hope that this is as bad as it gets, and the ice should help."

"Good thought, Professor. Thank you," responded James.

"This has been a good lesson for all of us. Don't leave the group unannounced. I know that I say that we should tally everything up to an adventure on this trip, but we don't need that kind of adventure again," I concluded with a slight grin.

If only I had known that our "adventures" had just begun.

CHAPTER 6

THIRD DAY IN PARIS

I arose by 10:00 that morning in order to find out how to contact the gendarmes. I explained the situation of James to the concierge, and he called the gendarmes' office to set up an appointment for 2:00 in the afternoon. We'd be done with class by then, and James could spend time describing what had happened to him.

The concierge – Monsieur Francois – said that he'd change James' and Rodney's room so that there would be no fear of a break-in.

"Don't worry about the lost key, Madame. It happens and we have extra keys. We may have the lock changed, though, in this case."

The hotel's breakfast hours were over before 10:00, and I knew of a bakery close by, so I went there to pick up two dozen croissants. I was sure that the students would be hungry and with tea and coffee always being served in the lobby, the delicious croissants would suffice. No one makes croissants better than the French.

By 11:00, word had gotten around that there was an abundance of croissants in the lobby, and everyone swarmed down to feast. Class started at noon, and the students seemed quiet and somber. I wondered for a moment if they were overwrought and perturbed with James for the unnecessary scare that he had caused, but soon I realized that they were still just a bit drained from the experience.

"James, how does your eye feel?" I asked when everyone was seated.

"It's fine. The ice helped a lot, so, again, thank you for the suggestion."

I nodded.

I introduced the next essay, which would be due the last day that we were in Paris. The essay was concerning one incident that had changed their views on an aspect of their lives in some way and why.

"I know that you are wondering if last night's incident could be used. Well, this topic was created when I was asked to teach this Study Abroad course, so I didn't plan it for the circumstance that occurred last night. In a word, 'yes' you may use it; however, I suggest that you wait to make sure that some other spectacle in Paris doesn't grab you."

James raised his hand. "I doubt that there will be anything in my lifetime that will change me as much as that foolish incident," he said, solemnly.

"Yes, I believe that it's safe to say that will probably be your topic, James," I answered with a grin. "Last year's group of students had their topic early on while in Paris," I continued.

"What happened?" asked Lisa.

"We got off the Metro at the Charles de Gaulle stop – same stop that we used this year – and we couldn't get out of the Metro. We just went in circles for about fifteen minutes when we finally concluded that we had exited the Metro train on the wrong side, and there was no exit where we were circling. We could see our exit, but we couldn't get to it. We'd have to leap the Metro wall."

"What!" exclaimed Lisa. "Seriously?"

"Yes, that's what we did. I helped everyone over the wall until I was the last one on the wrong side. The class helped pull me over to – by then – a group of astonished onlookers. It was hilarious and a bit embarrassing. I'll have a look on my phone. I may still have a picture for you to enjoy," I concluded with a broad smile.

We continued class with a lesson on the use of subordinate clauses and commas, the reading of journals, and then the sights that we would see for that afternoon.

"I had a variety of things on our list for today, but I've changed that as most of us are tired, so I thought that we should do just one sight – the Louvre – and I'll leave you to stay as long a time or as short as you want. I have only one request and that's that you stay in groups of two's or three's from now on."

They all nodded in agreement.

"When we get to the Louvre, I'll take you to the *Mona Lisa* and *Venus de Milo*, and then you'll be on your own. I've picked up brochures that will give ideas of artwork to see. I'll leave the brochures for you to pick up on your way out of the room. We won't leave here until 3:00, so you have time to freshen up if you wish.

* * * *

James told the gendarmes everything that happened and described the one culprit that he saw clearly. He was a scoundrel whom the police had been tracking for months, so this was no surprise to them. They expressed their regret that we had been involved with such a crowd, even though James personally took the blame.

I appointed Sara and Jessa to plan out our Metro route, which would actually be a quick ride to the Louvre.

As we exited the Metro, I pointed out Rue de Rivoli, a street with arcades, which housed shops, bookstores, department stores, and cafes.

"I love to stroll Rue de Rivoli because it has everything you could possibly want from Paris, and usually prices are good. Save time to shop if you so desire," I commented. "I know that I don't have to tell Sara that since she's the shopper of the group."

"I guess that I can't keep that a secret," she replied with a grin.

I led them to the Louvre, explaining as we walked that the museum contained one of the most important art collections in the world and had a history extending back to medieval times. It was first constructed as a fortress in 1190 and later became a palace and then a museum. Most recently the impressive glass pyramid entrance had been added, which allowed entrance to all of the galleries.

After showing them the *Mona Lisa* and *Venus de Milo*, I had a feeling that they would leave the Louvre exhausted as they all seemed mesmerized by everything we saw. I continued to say, "You can come back to this. Remember, it's by...."

I ended my session with the students by reminding them that class would start at 8:00 the next morning with journals due.

After leaving the students on their own, I strolled through the museum before I exited to visit some of my favorite shops on Rue de Rivoli. I grabbed an early dinner at one of my favorite restaurants – Sebillon – off the Champs Elysees. They always offered a variety of fish that was perfectly grilled, and then I headed to MacMahon Hotel to grade journals from yesterday's experiences.

I started grading in my room and, finally, decided to take all of my paraphernalia to the lobby where I could at least do a little people watching between grading sessions. Eventually, I took my work and walked to a delightful little café not far from the hotel and ordered a wine to finish up the grading...and then ordered another wine.

Now, I had the opportunity to just people watch. Indeed, the French were dressed up according to American standards. Many were walking arm-in-arm, older couples with canes still looking distinguished, some ladies strolling by in stilettos and light furs, a few men displaying a traditional beret, and tons of tourists looking like...well, like tourists.

And then my heart stopped. There was a man – totally out of place for the Champs Elysees crowd – with a raunchy beard, torn pants, and dingy shirt. No eye patch or long hair, but he was escorting a less-than-elegant lady, and I just got a tight feeling in my throat.

I watched as they continued down the boulevard and continued on past the MacMahon Hotel. *You've been watching too many scary movies*, I thought to myself. *This can't be the ruffian who punched James last night nor one of the prostitutes.*

However, having finished the journals, I asked for the bill, paid for the two wines, and returned to the hotel lobby. The wine had a way of calming my nerves, and I decided that seeing that hoodlum and possible prostitute was just coincidence. By 9:00, I decided to call it a day and returned to my room.

I arose at 6:30 to have breakfast and be ready for an early class at 8:00. Scarcely had I arisen than I got a knock at my door. Looking through the peep hole, I saw Lisa and Katie still in their pajamas and wearing distraught looks on their faces.

"Lisa...Katie, are you okay?" I asked as I quickly opened the door.

"No," Katie wailed. "We've been robbed."

CHAPTER 7

MURDER...SAY WHAT?

I nearly had to gasp for breath. "What!" was the only word that I could utter. "Come inside.

"When did this happen? Just now? Last night?"

"It was last night, but we don't know when. We were so tired," continued Lisa, "that we didn't notice anything out of place and just dropped onto our beds. Neither of us heard anything until we woke up this morning."

"Lisa's trying to say that it could have happened before we had returned to our room, but it could also have occurred during the night while we slept!" exclaimed Katie.

I put my hand to my mouth. "If that's true, then you are very lucky that you weren't attacked." I knew that they had already thought of this.

Another knock at the door. I looked at the girls, but they shrugged their shoulders.

Looking through the peep hole, I recognized one of the concierges that worked in the lobby.

"Good morning and excuse me, ladies," he started,

"there was an incident last night and there will be gendarmes in the hotel today. Nothing to worry about, but I wanted to warn you. Have you talked with all of your students yet?"

"Well, no, but Katie and Lisa have been robbed." I decided I should just blurt it out because the gendarmes would want a list of things that had been stolen.

"Oh, I'm so sorry," continued the concierge. "What is your room number? I'll send the gendarmes to your room."

"Room 501," stated Lisa. "We'll return there now if they want to talk with us."

Immediately, I made my rounds to the other rooms – first, James' and Rod's newly assigned room with Brad – to see if everyone was okay and nothing had been stolen from them. Everyone seemed fine.

The gendarmes were swarming through the halls, and I knew that this was not just a small incident – it was something serious.

I went to the front office to see Monsieur Francois, the concierge with whom I often chatted.

"Monsieur, what is happening? I'm in charge of nine students, and I don't want them in any danger."

"Yes, Madame, I know. I will tell you when all the information has been given to me, and I'm told that it's okay to talk to the people staying in our hotel. I'm sorry, but I can't say anything at the moment. I hope you understand, Madame."

"Promise that I'll be the first to know?"

"Yes, Madame."

At 8:00, everyone filed into the classroom except for Lisa and Katie, who were still talking with a team of gendarmes.

"What's happening?" asked Rodney.

"I don't know. Monsieur Francois promised to tell me when he could, so let's focus on our schoolwork. Do you have questions about the directions that I gave you for the essay?"

"May we write on more than one thing that has affected us?" asked Rita.

"I'd rather than you stuck to one topic...."

Just then, Lisa and Katie burst through the door.

"There's been a murder here!" exclaimed Katie.

"What! How do you know this?" I asked, panic entering my voice.

"We overheard a gendarme say that the body was cold and that he had been killed early last night. It was in a hushed whisper, but we both heard."

Chaos broke out in the classroom as I tried to settle everyone down.

"Listen, guys. If what you heard, ladies, is true, then the hotel employees will move all of us to another hotel. These things happen in big cities," I stammered, trying to keep my voice calm. "They happen in Chicago all of the time. It's just that we're not normally a part of the crime scene. By the time we're finished with class, I think that Monsieur Francois will have some concrete information. Now let's try to focus on our studies so that we can sightsee later."

It was difficult for all of us to concentrate, but I have to give the class credit – they really did try. By

10:00 when class was over, everyone bound out of the room and into the lobby as they knew that I was going to try to find Monsieur Francois.

"Madame, I was just about to come for you. Could we go to the back room to talk?"

I nodded and gave the class what I hoped was a positive smile.

"A man who was rooming alone was murdered last night while he was in bed. It seems to have been a robbery and the man must have awakened while the robbers were collecting their bounty. We believe that the same robbers also broke into the room of your two students, probably just before Monsieur Grande's room." He paused to catch his breath.

"It's a blessing that the girls were not in the room. We may have had more murders on our hands."

I was speechless – frantic at the thought. Immediately, I sent a prayer of thanks to God.

"Oh, how awful. What will we do now?" I asked since I couldn't think of anything else to say.

"We're moving everyone to our sister hotel on the Champs Elysees. It's much more expensive, but you will not be charged any extra. It's called Hotel Atala. If your students will pack all of their belongings into their bags, we'll take the responsibility of moving everything this afternoon, and you may collect your keys whenever you get to the hotel. Here is the address," he concluded, handing me their card.

"It's not a problem for us to take our suitcases over there, Monsieur."

"Madame, it's the least we can do. Everyone will

have the same roommate. Just tell the concierge what room you had been in here, and hand them the keys. He will, in turn, give you your new room along with the new keys."

After relaying the information to the class, they were noticeably upset with the concrete news of the murder and quickly dispersed to pack everything up. They met me in the lobby again at 11:00.

"Okay, class, let's walk to the Champs Elysees and locate the Hotel Atala and then have a bit of lunch before we start on our excursions. My plan is to go to Versailles and see the palace – a good idea since it will get us out of town for the afternoon."

* * * *

We took the train to Versailles. It gave us a chance to unwind after our horrendous morning, and I tried to get their minds off of things by telling them about Versailles.

"This palace is colossal – I don't know how else to describe it. Originally, there was a small hunting lodge on this property, but King Louis XIV rebuilt it into the largest palace in Europe, housing 20,000 people."

"You mean 2,000 people?" asked Sara.

"No, 20,000 people. It's immense." I paused for a moment to think. "The gardens to the palace are equally amazing as they were styled into geometric paths with hedges, flower beds, water pools, and fountains. When we get to the palace, we'll be given a map, but I'll tell you now that the most magnificent

HALL OF MIRRORS, VERSAILLES

room is the Hall of Mirrors. If we don't have time to get to everything, we definitely don't want to miss that room. I can't begin to explain it to you – you just have to see it."

"This is the palace that you stayed at when you came to Paris? You know, you were telling us about it the other day when we were still on the train," asked Carolyn.

I chuckled. "Well, we didn't stay at the palace – I could only wish! We stayed in the village of Versailles in one of the hotels."

Going to Versailles was the best place we could have gone. The students were entranced with the beauty, majesty, and display of money – which France couldn't afford at the time of Louis XIV – and, I believe, everyone temporarily forgot the dreadful morning.

* * * *

Fortunately, we had a few peaceful days in Paris. We did such things as visiting the Marais – an area of chic fashion boutiques, restaurants, and small art galleries – Place de Bastille, Musee Picasso, Pompidou Center, the Opera, the Tuileries, and dozens of sidewalk cafes to drink a cup of coffee or coke and people watch.

I returned to the MacMahon Hotel on the last day to ask Monsieur Francois if they had found the murderer.

"Yes, we believe so. He is a man from a bad area in Paris, and the gendarmes have been watching him for months. They are waiting for the results of the

DNA to come back before they can actually arrest him."

"Does he have a beard that is unkempt and shaggy and may sometimes wear a patch over his eye?" I questioned.

Monsieur Francois looked shocked. "Yes, you know him?"

"He is the fellow who robbed my student of the hotel key. I believe I saw him on the Champs Elysees on the night of the murder, except he didn't have the eye patch on."

"That eye patch is simply something that he puts on sometimes. You see, he doesn't have a real eye – just a glass one under the patch. He's a very bad criminal, and I hope that the gendarmes can book him," answered Monsieur Francois.

We left Paris on a good note. Yes, we had had problems at first, but we looked forward to days of carefree sightseeing in Amsterdam, and the worst was behind us. Or so we thought.

CHAPTER 8

FIRST DAY
IN AMSTERDAM

We took the train from Paris to Amsterdam. I tried to familiarize the students with some of the culture of The Netherlands.

"This land has a really rich history. Much of land in The Netherlands has been reclaimed from the sea in the last 300 years. Of course, the country is known for its windmills, which have drained the land and, thus, created fertile soil. Without the windmills and the rich soil, there would be no possibilities of farming. This farmland is called *polderland.*"

"Isn't it true," interrupted James, "that windmills also grind grain to make flour?"

"Exactly right, James. They also crush seeds to make oil. Now, do you see those canals that are running everywhere? The windmills drain the land, putting the water into the canals. The water is then carried by canal to rivers and then to the North Sea. It's quite interesting what these Dutch people have done to save their land."

WINDMILL, NETHERLANDS

"Is this country called The Netherlands or Holland?" asked Rita.

"Both," I answered. "Technically, it is The Netherlands, and only the northern region is Holland, but foreigners call the entire country Holland, so I guess you can say that the names are interchangeable."

"I remember a story my mother used to tell us about Holland. There was a little boy who put his finger into a dike to stop the sea from flooding the land," said Lisa with a smile.

"I remember that story as well," I commented.

"I haven't heard that story," remarked Brad. "What's a dike, exactly?"

"It's a high mound of land that stops water from flooding the countryside. They are quite high. Oh, look there. That's a dike," I said, pointing to the mound of land in the distance. "Anyway, on one of my trips to Holland, we went on a bike ride and rode on top of a dike. There are roads on the dikes as well."

"It would be fun to do a bike ride," inserted Jessa. "Is that possible for us?"

"Absolutely. I think that we were in Edam where they rented bikes by the hour. We'll check into that, class."

I stopped to think for a moment and then continued. "Going back to canals, here's a fun fact about them – they say that you can travel anywhere in Holland by canal. Every city or village is accessible by water. Kind of amazing, I think."

"How about those wind turbines that we see in the

States. Didn't they start here in The Netherlands?" questioned Rita.

"Oh, yes, they did. We'll see some along the way. They harness the really strong winds of this country to make electricity. They are sleek and beautiful to watch, but I really love to see those centuries-old windmills that still are working. We'll go to a village that has working windmills while we're in Holland."

We fell silent as we watched the beautiful scenery – fertile, green farmlands, lots of black and white cows, canals, and old-world farmhouses that had been standing for centuries.

"These farmhouses have been handed down from century to century to a family member. I understand that, if possible, farms all stay in the family forever. If there is no son or daughter in a farming family, then the house and land will go to a nephew or niece," I concluded.

I noticed everyone taking notes as I continued to give some of the history of Holland and then Amsterdam.

"We're within an hour from Amsterdam, so let me tell you a little about its founding. The city was founded as a small fishing village on the marshy mouth of the Amstel River. By the 17th century, Amsterdam was the center of a massive empire stretching across the world. The canal ring in Amsterdam along with the incredible gabled houses were constructed during the 16th and 17th centuries. Again, we are seeing old-world structures just as we saw in London and Paris.

"Let me tell you a little about the tulip since it was

and is still so significant in The Netherlands. Tulips were first cultivated in Turkey, and they were introduced to Holland during the 16th century. They sold for thousands of guilders – the currency at that time. People became obsessed with the tulip, and it caused what the Europeans called 'tulip mania'."

"Is the tulip the number one export product?" asked Jessa.

"Yes, it is, followed by chocolate."

"I just saw a sign for Rotterdam. Wasn't it completely bombed and leveled during WWII?" asked Rodney, the history buff.

"Sadly, yes, completely. It's a beautiful, modern city now with wide streets and huge shopping centers. So much different than the rest of Holland's old cities. But speaking of Rotterdam, let me tell you about a village that I once visited. I don't think that we'll have the opportunity to go there, but it's near Rotterdam. It's called Delfshaven. It has significant importance to us Americans because it is the port from which the Pilgrims left for the New World in 1620."

"Wait a minute," piped in Rodney. They left for the New World from England."

"Well, the Pilgrims originally left England in 1608 for Holland to escape religious persecution. When the children were becoming 'too Dutch,' they thought that they needed to seek refuge in the New World."

"Really!" exclaimed Rodney. "I totally didn't know that. They lived in Holland for a while before moving to America?"

I nodded. "They were in Holland for ten years, actually. They left this country from the village of Delfshaven and worshiped in the church there at the port. Some say that they actually slept in the old church their last night in Holland, but that has never been proven. The church is now called 'The Pilgrim Fathers' Church.' It's really astonishing.

"However, you're right, Rodney. The pilgrims left Delfshaven on the Speedwell – a boat that proved to be unseaworthy – and went back to England. As you already know, they ended up crossing the Atlantic on the *Mayflower*, landing at Plymouth, Massachusetts in 1620."

"If we have time, could we visit there?" questioned James. "That would be so interesting."

"I doubt that we'll have time, plus there is no bus or train that goes to Delfshaven. I'm sorry. We'll see many interesting sights, so don't worry about that. Holland is packed with incredible old-world villages, and Amsterdam has amazing sights as well. First on our list will be Anne Frank's house."

I paused for a moment. "Now, I'm going to be quiet and work on grading the essays that you handed in this morning," I commented with a grin.

* * * * *

By the time the train reached Central Station in Amsterdam, I had worked my way through two essays. I quickly put my schoolwork away and focused on one of my favorite cities in Europe. If you ask any Dutchman how he would rate the three big cities in

The Netherlands, he would probably say, "Rotterdam is the city to work in; The Hague is the city to live in; but Amsterdam is the city to play in."

"Gather your bags and get ready to see one of the most interesting places on the continent. We're going to take the tram to our hotel – The Museum Hotel."

"Tram?" questioned Carolyn. "Is that like a streetcar?"

"Yes, exactly. Again, beware of pickpockets in the train station. Remember, watch out for each other. I'll lead the way to our tram, and James bring up the rear."

It was a short hike to the tram station, and we boarded Tram 17 that would take us near our hotel. I watched the students as they got their first sight of Amsterdam with the centuries-old canal houses, and I had to smile. They reminded me of myself as I got my first glimpse and said that the houses looked like "gingerbread houses" from a fairytale.

As we entered the Museum Hotel, I went straight to the clerk, and everyone flopped on the sofas and chairs arranged in the lobby. As the clerk got our keys readied, I handed out the tram maps and explained to the students how they worked. It was more complicated than the metros that we had encountered in both London and Paris, but if they stayed in twos, I had confidence that two minds would be better than one. At least that was my *hope*.

I handed out the keys and pointed to the small elevator. "You're used to small elevators, right?" I asked with a grin. "There's a significant difference, though

– the stairs are very steep and winding. There are lights at the bottom of the stairs and on each floor. Turn them on and they will turn themselves off after an allotted time."

"Well, another culture change, right?" chimed in Sara. "We like learning the new traditions of each country."

"Well, let's get started. I'll hand you your key, get your suitcases loaded onto the elevator, and find your room. In half an hour, be back down here for class. That door over there," I said, pointing to a red door in the lobby, "is for the room that we'll use for class. We'll have our discussion before we head out to Anne Frank's house. Remember, your journals are due for the last day in Paris."

* * * * *

Our class time lasted two hours, and by then, it was 1:00.

"Let's grab some lunch so that I can fill you in on a few details about Anne Frank before we visit her house. We'll walk over to Hard Rock Café, and you can grab a hamburger and fries – America style," I concluded.

Before we got a seat, the class wanted a Hard Rock t-shirt or some memento of our visit. After finding a large table and ordering, I gave them a few facts about Anne.

"As you know, Anne was Jewish, and her family came to Holland from Germany in search of a safe country. In 1941, the Germans took over Holland, and

CANALS OF AMSTERDAM

ANNE FRANK HOUSE, AMSTERDAM

Anne and her family went into hiding upstairs in her father's spice factory. Eventually, Anne and her family were captured and sent to a concentration camp. The only one to survive was her father. We'll be visiting that spice factory with the hiding place upstairs," I concluded.

"How did they get caught?" questioned Rita.

"They believe that one of the workers from the spice factory found out about the hiding place and turned them in for a small amount of money. People were starving in The Netherlands, so people were desperate for any money that they could get. It was a dire situation, but I can't imagine turning someone in for pocket change. However, there were many more people who were good Dutch citizens who joined the resistance movement and hid Jewish people, fed them, and helped them escape."

By then the burgers and fries had arrived, and the students dug in. By 2:30, we were ready to walk to 263 Prinsengracht to see Anne's hiding place.

* * * *

It was nearly dark when we finally emerged from the spice factory and hiding place, and I suggested that we go on a canal ride to see Amsterdam at its best – alit with thousands of lights. It was a grand finale to a most perfect day – businesses, bridges, house boats, and monuments were all lighted. I left the class together at the Leidseplein, a popular place to get a snack and drinks.

"Our hotel is just over the bridge here, and I suggest you don't stay long as we have a full schedule tomorrow. We're going to catch a bus to an old fishing village called Volendam and then go to Edam to rent bikes. Our class period will be at 8:00."

The students' eyes lit up with the mention of the bikes, and I bid them good night. I was hoping for a peaceful night, but that wasn't the case.

CHAPTER 9

GOING FURTHER AFIELD

After staying up half the night grading essays, it was difficult to adhere to my alarm clock going off at 6:30.

"Ugh," I sighed as I turned off the alarm and closed my eyes to the world. At 6:45 I finally rolled out of bed, took a quick shower, applied a little make-up, and headed for the breakfast bar. Silently, I again thanked my hairdresser for the no-mess, no-fuss haircut that needed only to be washed and a comb whisked through it. I had a fairly leisurely breakfast and headed for the classroom.

I normally started class with questions from the previous day's activities.

Jessa raised her hand. "This has something to do with last night. We saw our first mime, and he was fascinating. You'll have to ask Carolyn about it, though."

"Oh? Carolyn, what happened?"

She giggled. "Well, this mime would strike a stance and then stand perfectly still for two or three minutes while people would put money into his hat. Then suddenly he would move to shake hands with whoever was in front of him. Well, I put money into his hat, and he held out his hand to shake mine – only he wouldn't let go of my hand. He just kept shaking it."

The class was laughing, remembering the incident.

"I kept trying to get away, but he held tighter. I was laughing so hard that I gave up trying to get him to release me."

"Obviously, he finally did," I said with a chuckle.

Carolyn nodded, still laughing.

"Mimes are very entertaining, and I'm surprised that we didn't see any until now. However, you did get a good taste of one last night, I guess."

"Another thing that I noticed," added James, "is that the Dutch are far more friendly than the English or French. I mean, the French were better than the English, but the Dutch actually smile and talk to us. They act like 'real' people, you know."

"Yes, they not only speak English as their second language, but also they are more Americanized than some of the other Europeans. I've asked them about this, and they claim it's because of American television shows that they watch." I explained.

I handed back their essays and we talked about them. We did a quick lesson in grammar covering some of their mistakes I found in the essays. The students read from their journals, and then we discussed our day's itinerary.

"First, class, we're taking a bus from the Central Station to Volendam. It's an old fishing village on the Zuiderzee, which is an inlet from the North Sea. Many tourists now visit Volendam because of its authenticity. You'll see some people wearing the traditional Dutch costumes – women in black blouses, lace-winged caps, striped aprons, and wooden shoes; men in black baggy pants, sweaters, and a neckerchief. It's quite interesting. One of the stores offers to take your photo in costumes if you wish.

"We'll spend an hour there and then take the bus to Edam, which is nearby. It's known throughout the world for its ball-shaped cheeses that are wrapped in red wax. Edam is exceptionally lovely, full of narrow streets and canals and bordered by elegant, gabled houses from the 16th century. The canals are crossed by real drawbridges that must be raised in order to let boat traffic pass. It's quite interesting."

"And we'll have time to ride a bike?" asked Sara.

"Yes, we'll allow time for that. I want you to go home saying that you rode on top of a dike," I commented.

"Then I think we'll have time to catch a bus to Zaanse Schans where the working windmills are grinding cacao to make chocolate, grains to make flour, and seeds to make oil. One of the mills is generating power, too, for the village. The people of the village are dedicated to preserving the traditional Dutch way of life, and Zaanse Schans is run as a piece of living history. You'll love the village. Now, any questions?"

"Are there souvenir shops," asked Sara quite seriously.

The class laughed because they knew of Sara's love of souvenirs. How she would get everything into her one bag to go home waits to be seen. Right now, she has several other girls helping her carry her loot.

VOLENDAM, THE NETHERLANDS

"Of course, Sara. They are constructed just for you! Okay, you have ten minutes to go to your room to ditch your class material and grab your journal notebook. See you here in the lobby."

* * * *

When we got to Volendam, I designated a meeting place to convene in an hour. I stopped for a cup of coffee at one of the outdoor cafes and then meandered down the main street of Volendam. The village had always been a favorite of mine while in Holland. I saw most of the students crammed inside of the photographer's shop to dress in the native costumes and get their pictures taken.

"Professor Kira!" It was Carolyn who called me with fear in her voice.

"What is it, Carolyn? Has something happened?"

"Yes. My money is gone. I went to get my wallet out when we were waiting in line at the photographer's shop, and it's gone. It must have happened last night."

"Oh, dear, when you were engaged with the mime!" I exclaimed.

"Just like you said – pickpockets distract you and then steal."

"Yes, but I doubt that the mime was involved. Often, pickpockets just look for an opportunity. Did you have a credit card in your wallet? How much money?"

"Fortunately, I didn't have too much money in the wallet. Most of my money, passport, and credit card were in my waist-wallet that was hidden under my clothes."

"Smart girl," I added.

By then, I saw a look of distress on Sara's face, and I felt sure there had been a second robbery.

"Sara," I whispered, "has someone robbed you?"

"Yes, how did you know?"

"By the look on your face. Plus, Carolyn is in the same situation. I think it happened while all of you were entranced by the mime. What are you missing?"

"Oh, my gosh, Professor Kira. They got most of the money that I had left for the trip along with my passport!" Sara was in tears.

"Okay, now don't panic. Did you make a copy of your passport as I told everyone to do?"

"Yes, it's in my suitcase."

"Okay, after our trip to Edam and the bike ride, I'll take everyone to Zaanse Schans, and you and I will go to the hotel to get your photocopy and then head to the American Embassy to get you a temporary passport. Meanwhile, I need to make sure that the other girls haven't been robbed."

* * * *

Everyone else was safe, but it put the entire class on high alert now that two of the girls had been robbed.

"I feel terrible, Professor Kira," interrupted Katie. "You told us to watch out for each other, and we all were just sitting there watching the mime."

"Don't blame yourself," I added. "It was an entertaining performance that you hadn't seen before, and that sort of thing can happen. Each of you girls should keep your purses on your laps when you're sitting, and guys keep everything important in your front pockets. I think that most of you have either a waist-wallet or a small pouch that hangs from your neck and is hidden. Use them as much as you can. Keep your passports in there as well."

At the end of the hour, we caught a bus to Edam and enjoyed the beauty of the small village. The rented bikes were right outside of the centrum – the main part of the old-city – and we rode for an hour. On top of the dike, all we could see on both sides were the blue ripples of water. The students stopped to take pictures as the wind blew from the nearby North Sea and as the sun reflected its golden rays off the Zuiderzee.

We found the bus that would go to Zaanse Schans, and it was in Zaanse Schans that Sara and I left the group and headed into Amsterdam and the American Embassy – not before pointing out the windmills and especially showing them the one in which they could climb up to the blades of the windmill. I knew that they would enjoy that.

"All of you meet back here in an hour or so, and take bus 11 that will go into Amsterdam. It will let you off at the Central Station and you can either walk to the hotel or take bus 17. Questions?"

With no questions, I added, "We'll meet you back at the hotel around dinner time, and stay together," I concluded.

Sara and I bid the class good-bye and headed into Amsterdam, going directly to the hotel for her photocopy of her passport and then on to the American Embassy. It wasn't a big deal to get a temporary passport, and with a relieved Sara, we returned to the hotel.

"How much money do you have left?" I asked Sara. "Do you want to borrow some from me?"

"No, I just need to stop buying souvenirs for everyone back home."

"I know you have three or four siblings that you're probably buying for, and you're welcome to borrow from me because who knows if you'll return, and, I admit, there are tons of unique items that are difficult to resist."

"Well, if I see something that I can't put down, I'll let you know. As you have already pointed out, I have more souvenirs than anyone else in the class," Sara concluded with a smile.

Everyone returned safely, and dinner was at the Leidseplein. The class had enjoyed their evening there the night before, and it was one of the best places in Amsterdam to eat and be entertained.

Before long, a mime appeared. She was the Statue of Liberty – dressed totally in gold with even her skin painted gold— and she only moved her head slightly when someone put money in her container. The class was again fascinated by the perfect stillness of the mime. However, this time the girls held tightly to their purses.

While eating, we discussed the next day's itinerary.

"Tomorrow is Friday, and we're going to see a performance that takes place only on Fridays."

"What is it?" The class was excited.

"It's the Alkmaar cheese market. I say 'performance' because the cheese is carried by two porters on a sled-like affair, which is loaded with eighty cannon-ball-sized cheeses. A leather shoulder sling is attached to the sled's handles, so the two porters can carry it between them. It's pretty awesome."

I stopped to think what else I needed to tell them to prepare them for the market. "Oh, yes, the porters are dressed in spotless, white costumes with lacquered, brightly-colored straw hats. They kind of glide with the sleds and put on a unique performance for the audience.

"And then on Saturday, we'll stay in Amsterdam again and visit the Rijksmuseum, which is right by our hotel. You can almost see it from here," I said, pointing in the direction of the museum. "You'll see Rembrandt's *The Night Watch*, which is one of the most exquisite pieces of art in the museum. In the afternoon, I'll take you to an open market. They are so popular in Europe, and I can seldom pass one up. You'll not only find treasures there but also items that stores sell but for a much cheaper price at the market. Also, you can bargain with some of the merchants to get the price lower," I added with a smile.

"I'm keeping Sunday a secret for the moment because it's our last day in Holland. However, I should mention your next essay because you'll be working on it Sunday afternoon and evening. You already know the topic – how have I changed during this European adventure? – and you need to be getting your rough draft started now.

"I think that we're all totally different people than when we left the States a short three weeks ago," chimed in James. "I hardly recognize myself," he concluded with a grin.

"Yes, you are, and now you have to put that into a well-organized essay," I concluded.

"Okay, I believe that I'm going to walk to the hotel. I have journals to grade. You need to watch out for each other and come along soon. You have a journal plus an essay to do, and we have another busy day ahead of us."

Could we have a night without any mishaps or adventures? I thought to myself silently. Probably not, I decided, but I forced myself to think positively.

CHAPTER 10

ALKMAAR AND ZUIDERZEE MUSEUM AND OFF-THE-BEATEN PATH IN AMSTERDAM

I stopped at an automatic machine to get bus tickets for tomorrow's trip to Alkmaar – all paid for by Bradley through their students' fees – and deposited them into my purse. I had had extra money for "special" things that the students had wanted to do, such as the bike ride. I had enough left from that allowance for one more small experience. We could use that on Saturday when we were in Amsterdam. It was a city packed with fun things to do, and it wouldn't be difficult to spend the last of our allowance.

"You're alone?" asked a male voice behind me.

My heart stopped, realizing for the first time that I had told students never to be alone.

"Yes," I answered with what I hoped was a strong, forceful voice. "What do you want?"

"What do you have?"

I turned to see a police officer facing me. "You're police?" I asked, trying to decide if he was real or a robber in disguise.

"Yes, Mevrouw, and I'm wishing that you had a partner and weren't walking alone," he answered, flashing his ID at me.

I let out an audible sigh of relief, but my heart was still pounding.

"Oh, I tell my students to walk in pairs, and here I am all alone. I'm just walking back to the hotel, and well, uhm, could you please accompany me?"

Was it my imagination or was my voice shaking, too?

"My pleasure, Mevrouw."

"Thank you," I said. "I'm teaching a group of students from an American university. It's a Study Abroad course."

"Well, you need to take the advice that you give out to your class about walking by yourself at night. There are many drug dealers on the streets at night. We like to think that Amsterdam is a safe place, but often at night, things get a little crazy. At least you're not in the Red Light District," he said with a grin.

I nodded as we passed the Rijksmuseum, lit up in all its grandeur.

"There's the Museum Hotel, and that's where we're staying." I stated as I pointed down the street. "I want to thank you, Sir."

"Well, you didn't have far to go, but still remember your own advice."

"Will do. Thank you again," I said as I shook his hand.

As I entered the lobby of the hotel, I had to sit in the first chair I saw as now I found that my legs were shaky. *How could I have been so foolish to walk alone?* I questioned myself.

* * * *

Normally, we had a two-hour class, but this Friday was only an hour long as we had to catch a bus to Alkmaar and be on time for the selling of the cheese. When we arrived in Alkmaar, we went straight to the historic center of town as the bidding and selling of the cheese had already begun. The students loved watching the porters carrying the balls of cheese on the sleds. It was always done with such precision, and the crowds totally enjoyed their performance.

There was an open market surrounding the cheese market, selling everything from balls of cheese to local handmade pottery. It was an ideal market with so much local merchandise that they hadn't seen anywhere else. We spent an hour just perusing the market and buying trinkets – because that's all they had room for in their suitcases – to take home. I asked Sara again if she needed some money, but she declined.

"You know," I commented when we still had a free afternoon ahead of us, "I think that we have time to take a bus to the Zuiderzee Museum, which is just north of here. It's an entire outside village made into a museum, showing things from all over Holland."

"That sounds unique and fun," commented Rita. "Let's do it."

The bus ride was a short one, and we saw sights replicated from all over The Netherlands in this open-air museum, including a fishing village from the north, a working windmill, the smoking of fish, a sail-maker's shop, and a centuries-old church. The weather was perfect, and everyone seemed to really enjoy being outdoors at this unique museum.

After a couple of hours at the outdoor museum, we caught a bus that went directly from the museum to the Central Station of Amsterdam.

"I know that all of you have journals and an essay to work on, so how about we split up here. From the conversations that I've heard on the bus, some of you want to get something to eat and some of you want to go back to the hotel to work. Of course, I have journals to grade, so splitting up might be the way to go. Now, all of you know the way back to the hotel, right?"

"Yes, we are experts on finding our way around Amsterdam. Well, at least we know the way to our hotel from here. We might get a bit confused if we went further afield," announced James with a smile.

"Okay, then I'll see you at 8:00 tomorrow morning for class, and....well, who remembers where we're going tomorrow?"

"Uhm, the museum where *The Night Watch* is displayed, but I forgot the name," chimed in Rita.

"Correct. It's the Rijksmuseum, near our hotel. And where else?"

"I'm probably wrong," inserted Lisa, "but shopping?"

Everyone laughed.

"Actually, she is correct," I commented, "because we're going to the Albert Cuypstraat open market. I just want you to see a very large open market where you can buy almost anything. Maybe you'll just buy candy, but it's worth seeing. It's where many locals buy merchandise rather than spending too much at an expensive department store.

"Okay, I'll see you in the morning at 8:00," I concluded.

* * * *

The next morning, I entered the breakfast room of the Museum Hotel at 7:00 to a crowded table of students engrossed in a quiet conversation but with a mayhem of laughter from time to time.

Oh, boy, I thought. *Something happened last night.* I counted heads, and everyone was present, so that wasn't a problem. Brad and Rodney were doing most of the talking – rather whispering – with James chiming in here and there.

I had my suspicions, but I decided to wait until class time, and, surely, I'd hear of the escapade.

I always started with comments about the previous day, and I could tell that everyone was trying to hide a smile or laugh. However, everyone kept silent.

"Well, from what I observed in the breakfast room, there must have been exorbitant excitement – all the whispering and chaotic laughing. Don't I get to laugh, too?" I questioned, trying to act hurt.

"I believe that this is Brad's story," said Rita.

"Brad? Quiet, innocent Brad?" I asked, amazed.

"I'm not going to get into trouble, am I?" Brad questioned.

"Well, it depends. You didn't hook up with the police last night, did you?"

"No, no, we didn't," commented James. "Go ahead, Brad, spill the beans."

"Well, you see, we were eating with some boys about our age who were from Amsterdam. We told them the things that we had seen, and they immediately asked why we hadn't gone to see the Red Light district."

Hilarious laughter filled the room, and I nodded my head.

"I had an idea that that's what you were going to say when I saw you three boys leading the conversation this morning," I said, smiling. "Well, tell us about it, and then maybe I can add some facts to the list of things that you saw to make it interesting enough to be in your journals tomorrow."

Brad started, "Well, the girls were actually standing in the windows – which went all the way to the floor – pretty much totally nude. They stood in unique poses that begged for...well, for business. This is very difficult to explain – and embarrassing."

Some of the girls were holding their sides from all of the laughter.

"Well, I have to retract my earlier statement in asking if you had gotten into trouble with the cops to 'did you give them any business?'"

The class broke out in uproarious laughter as the boys shook their heads.

"No, we just looked," commented James, still laughing.

"All three of you boys were there?"

"Yep, we were," answered Rodney.

"Why did you think that Brad should tell the tale then?" I asked.

"It was his idea," chimed in Rodney as well as James.

"Oh, I see. Well, it is a sight to behold, I must admit. You won't see anything like it in, say, Chicago. But let me give you some facts about prostitution in The Netherlands. Would you like that?"

"Sure," answered Rodney.

"If I remember correctly, prostitution in Amsterdam extends back to the 13th century when the city emerged as a seaport. Sea-weary sailors, well, you know...." I tried to gather my thoughts and present them professionally. "The prostitutes were supposed to conduct their 'business' in this one area – by the way, ironically, it's next to the oldest church in Amsterdam – and by the mid-17th century, prostitution was openly tolerated."

"So the people of Holland had no complaint about prostitution?" asked Jessa.

"Well, yes, some of the protestants tried to outlaw it, but attempts were met halfheartedly by the police, and, well, you can see what happened in the end.

Now there are not only prostitutes, but also garish sex shops, junkies, dealers, and lots of pickpockets in this area of Amsterdam."

"Yes, we saw all of that, too," chimed in Rodney again with a grin on his face.

"You didn't get pickpocketed, did you, boys? It's prevalent in that area."

"Not that we know of," answered Brad.

"Well, I don't know that I can top this escapade of last night, but let's hear what you wrote in your journals."

CHAPTER 11

AMSTERDAM IS ANYTHING BUT BORING

By 11:00 we found ourselves at the famous Rijksmuseum only a block or so from our hotel.

After buying our passes for the museum, I stood in the grand entrance to tell the students a little about the galleries.

"I've been told that this world-famous museum has the most complete and unrivaled collection of Dutch paintings from around the 15th to 19th century. I want to take you to that wing of the museum so that you don't miss that collection, and then we'll split up. The section that we'll see together contains the paintings of Vermeer and Rembrandt. So here we go," I concluded, guiding them toward the wing to the right.

We toured the wing for half an hour before we entered the gallery with Rembrandt's *The Night Watch*. The painting remarkably takes up most of a wall. With a large bench in front of the painting, I saw

Lisa and Carolyn literally fall onto it, their eyes enormous and their mouths open.

I giggled. "You know, girls, that's exactly how I reacted the first time I saw *The Night Watch*. I expected it to be the size of...oh, let's say, the *Mona Lisa*. And here was this gigantic, spectacular painting of 17th-century drama."

"I have no words for this," stammered Lisa.

"Definitely, something like I've never seen in my life," chimed in Carolyn.

"I know that you probably have room for a print of this in your suitcase, Lisa, so if you don't have the money, you know I'll lend you some. When I saw it the first time, I went to the counter and bought a canvas of it. When I got home, I spent a fortune having it stretched and then framed, but I didn't care. It's the most spectacular item that I have in my house. At least, that's what I think," I concluded.

"Surely, it's not that size," commented Lisa.

"No, no. It's probably 30-by-20 or something like that. However, it's magnificent."

"Yes, I'll have to have a print. I'll check on the cost, but I think I can afford it," concluded Lisa.

As the other students stood staring at the grandeur of *The Night Watch*, I told them that I'd meet them outside of the museum at 2:00. We could do a quick late lunch and then head for the open market.

* * * *

By 2:00, everyone was starving, and the Hard Rock Café was just across the street. It was time for another

REMBRANDT'S "THE NIGHT WATCH"

American lunch, and an outdoor table allowed us the opportunity to watch the canal boats cruise up and down the canal.

"You know, I have a little money left that we can do one more activity, and I'm wondering if you'd like to take another canal boat ride this evening. If we get on at a different dock than we did last time, we can see entirely different sights. What do you think?"

It was pretty much unanimous to do just that. I had enough money to afford the special wine-and-cheese cruise so that would make it especially unique and memorable.

"And when we're done eating, I have an idea of how to get to Albert Cuypstraat market," I said.

"Something besides walking or taking a tram?" questioned Rodney.

I nodded. "Have you noticed the bikes that have a little carriage behind them for people to ride?"

"Oh, yeah!" Rodney exclaimed. Everyone was talking at once now, and I knew that we had discovered a new mode of transportation.

After the students finished their burgers, fries, and shakes plus bought a few more keychains saying, "Hard Rock Amsterdam," we went to the area offering the "bike taxis."

It was a fun and interesting ride. You can literally see anything in Amsterdam – we passed several women dressed in stylish dresses and stilettos who were walking the cobblestone alleys where three homeless men were lying in doorways. We saw several men standing at the edge of a canal, urinating into it. The most unique image, though, was a man dressed in his wedding dress and throwing small bouquets into the crowd following him. I assumed that one of the men in the crowd was his "husband."

We arrived at the Albert Cuypstraat market all the wiser for having taken a bike taxi.

"Wow, we got to see some entertaining areas on that ride," commented Jessa. "Much more interesting than taking the tram."

"Virtually any encounter is possible in Amsterdam."

I thought for a moment. "Well, let me tell you a little about this market. I already told you that you can buy nearly anything here from fish, poultry, cheese, and vegetables to clothes, fabric, watches, postcards, and trinkets. The stallholders say that the Albert Cuypstraat market is the best in all of Europe.

"Oh, and this street we're standing on used to be a canal. When the market holders decided to make a huge open market in this area, they had to reconstruct the canal into a wide boulevard so that the market could serve this entire side of Amsterdam with food and everyday goods. Now, however, it serves about 20,000 visitors each day and twice that many on weekends."

We spent the next two hours perusing the market and sat for a cup of coffee at one of the outdoor cafes to just people-watch. Again, we saw a diverse array of people.

We took the opportunity to return to the centrum of Amsterdam via bike-taxi and stopped at Kalverstraat – a pedestrian boulevard with no cars allowed – where we shopped at the latest fashion stores.

"I'm going back to the hotel for awhile to grade. The wine-and-cheese canal cruise won't take place until it's dark. We can leave from the boat dock at the end of Kalverstraat," I said, pointing to the end of the street where several boats were moored. "Let's meet there at 9:00 tonight. How does that sound?"

"Great," chimed in James. "I'm already hungry again so eating is first on my list."

"Okay. Everyone just stay out of trouble. We're in our last days, and I think that we have had enough adventures. Some of you probably need to work on your essay or journal."

I returned to my hotel room to grab the essays and seated myself outside of the hotel at a small cafe to grade, breathe in the fresh air, and observe the people from time to time.

* * * *

By 9:00 all of us were gathered at the boat dock at the end of Kalverstraat. I saw no one with packages so they either didn't shop or they had returned to the hotel to dispose of their belongings.

"I see that everyone is here…that's a plus," I commented with a chuckle. "This is a really special tour because not only do we get wine and cheese on the tour, but also we have candlelight on each of our tables. And mid-way through the tour, we'll stop at a pub and get a glass of wine or soft drink there as well."

"This is awesome. We're all so excited because we

loved the last canal tour, and this one sounds just...
well, just enchanting," said Carolyn.

It was a three-hour tour. We had made a half-hour
stop at a pub for our wine and listened to some au-
thentic old Dutch music. Getting back onto the boat,
we started off slowly, winding through a beautifully
lit area. Then we made a sharp turn, there it was –
the Red Light district.

"I had no idea that we would get a chance to see
this district a second time," whispered James. "Did
you, Professor Kira?"

A little stunned that the canal trip offered its own
view of the Red Light district – but why should I be
because the least expected sights are feasible in Amsterdam – I replied, "No, I had no idea. However,
you're now getting a canal-side view of the girls."

The barely clad prostitutes were all bathed in a
pale red neon light as they made suggestive signs to
attract attention and garner customers for business.

The university girls – seeing the prostitutes for a
first time – were a bit dumbfounded by the entire
scene.

"Well, class, all I can say is that we are seeing one
of the defining images of modern-day Amsterdam."

CHAPTER 12

HEADING BACK TO LONDON

I had designated class for 3:00 in the afternoon on Sunday as we were going to church in the morning. I kept this as a surprise for the students because it wasn't just any church – it was the church in which the pilgrims worshiped during their stay in Amsterdam. The only English church in Amsterdam, it was located in an area named the Begijnhof.

The Begijnhof was built in 1346 and housed a sanctuary of unwed ladies – a lay Catholic sisterhood who lived like nuns but took no monastery vows. These ladies undertook the work of educating the poor and looking after the sick.

The Begijnhof is cut off from the bustling traffic of Amsterdam with a sanctified atmosphere, allowing the tourists and onlookers the certainty of being on holy ground. The beautiful, old houses are built in a square shape with a gorgeous flower garden in the center and the English Reformed Church on one end.

"We're going to worship where the pilgrims worshiped?" asked Lisa, enthusiastically.

I nodded.

"This is so exciting!" exclaimed Rodney. "Let's go."

"Wait, wait. Not so fast. I want to tell you about the church. It was built in the early 15th century, and in 1920, a church in Chicago dedicated a stained-glass window depicting the pilgrim fathers kneeling to pray in Delfshaven before boarding the Speedwell."

"And we'll see this window?" asked Rita.

"Yes, it's gorgeous and truly depicts the pilgrims just as they looked. I wanted this excursion to be a surprise to all of you because I know that you wanted to go to Delfshaven, which wasn't possible, but this is second best."

"I think it'll be equal to the missed adventure to Delfshaven since the pilgrim fathers called this their place of worship. I'm really excited," stated Rodney. "I know that I'm a foolish history buff, but I love that you're taking us there."

"Do they speak Dutch or what? How will we understand the sermon?" asked Katie.

"Oh, it's the English Reformed Church, and only English is spoken. It accommodates the Americans and English people who live in Amsterdam. Well, okay, I think that Rodney is just chomping at the bit, so we'd better go!"

The weather was perfect, so we opted to walk to the church. It was a bit of a hike, but we walked next to a canal and watched the ducks, geese, and swans as they searched for food.

"I would have saved that extra piece of bread that I didn't need," commented Rita, "if I had known we'd see so many beautiful swans on the canal."

The students were awestruck by the beauty of the Begijnhof.

"It's totally silent in here," whispered Jessa. "How can the Kalverstraat be right next door, and we don't hear the pedestrians talking and laughing?"

"Incredible, huh?" I asked. "And if you look at house number 34, it's the oldest wooden house in all of Amsterdam."

Upon entering the church, the students' eyes went directly to the stained-glass window of the pilgrim fathers. It was even more beautiful than I had remembered. We sat so that all could have an excellent view of the window.

The church service was amazing as the pastor talked about being humble, and humility was something that we all battled against at one time or another.

We exited the church around noon.

"On Sundays, there's usually a small open market right outside of the Begijnhof. They have very unusual items, and all are handmade locally. Let's have a look," I suggested.

We perused the open market, and I found a hand-painted gold, black, and white scarf that I couldn't live without. I had bought very little on this trip, so I couldn't pass up something that was love at first sight.

An outdoor café begged us to stop for a bite to eat before we headed back to the hotel so the students could work on their final essay.

"I know I said that the essays would be due at 6:00 tonight, but I could make it tomorrow morning before we leave for the ferry to take us back to London. Would that be better for you?"

There was a consensus of opinion that the new deadline would be perfect, so anyone who wanted could get up early to finish the essay and, thus, have a final evening visit to Leidseplein before leaving the incredible city of Amsterdam.

* * * *

We met up at 8:00 to catch a tram to the Central Station, and from there, we got a train to Hoek van Holland. I collected the final essays on the train and watched as the amazing countryside of The Netherlands slipped by outside of our train windows.

"I loved this country," commented Lisa. "The countryside was beautiful; we got to see the North Sea; and, most importantly, the people were open and friendly."

"I agree," chimed in Rita. "I believe that this was my favorite country of the three."

"We haven't finished yet with England," I said with a smile. "We are going to Canterbury tomorrow on the train. It's an incredible city. Just wait and see."

At Hoek van Holland, we caught the ferry to Harwich, England. From there we took a train to London.

"The Chunnel was so much faster, but I really enjoyed being on the English Channel. I felt as if I were on the North Sea," commented Rodney.

"Yes, if you're going to England from Paris, the

Chunnel is the way to go. Well, you had two totally different experiences, so that was kind of cool," I said, as we sat in our seats on the Tube. "We're headed back to St. Giles Hotel, so you'll be in familiar territory. You'll hand in one more journal tomorrow when we get onto the plane heading home.

"Here's what I suggest – even though you didn't ask me," I said with a chuckle. "You need to arrange your suitcase tonight because tomorrow will be a long day. You'll have time on the train from Canterbury back to London to write your journal, but it'll be a late night and an early-morning start to get to the airport.

"Okay, we have two more stops till we get to our destination at Russell Square, so gather up your belongings," I concluded.

Checking into the hotel was much easier the second time around. The students took the same rooms that they had previously occupied, and since they knew their way around London, I left them to themselves. I had essays to grade, and – after a word of warning to stay in pairs and watch out for each other – I bid them adieu with the reminder that we'd leave in the morning at 8:00.

My evening was uneventful – as I hoped the students' evening was – as I went to a nearby café and sat in the cool evening air and graded papers. Finally, by 9:00, I moved into the lobby of the hotel, and finally at 11:00, I called it a night. I had finished all of the papers except for a few journals that I had decided I'd finish on our way to Canterbury.

I was a bit worried when at 7:00, I saw no students in the breakfast room. Were they still sleeping? Had they already eaten? Were they in the hotel at all or still "out on the town"? My mind began to create horrible possibilities. I decided to go to Lisa's and Katie's room to check on them.

Lisa had obviously still been sleeping when she opened the door.

"Oh, Professor Kira. What time is it?"

"Lisa, we catch the train in an hour. Get up. I better check on everyone else. Is everyone okay?" I questioned as a last-minute thought.

"It was a bad night for all of us. We'll tell you on the train," stated Lisa, tiredly.

At each door, it was the same — everyone was still in bed. *Wow,* I thought, *good thing I was up and concerned about them, but what did Lisa mean that it had been a bad night?*

CHAPTER 13

ON OUR WAY TO CANTERBURY

Miraculously, everyone was ready at 8:00 but with no breakfast. The breakfast bars that they had brought from the States would have to suffice. I didn't ask any questions on the Tube as we headed to the train station, but once we were seated on the train, I began my inquiry.

"What happened last night? Obviously, you didn't get much sleep because you guys look terrible."

There was silence for a while, and then James decided he would start the story.

"Well, unfortunately, we all went to a pub in Soho."

"Oh, that can be a shady area, you know."

"Yes, well, we found that out. We were just going to get one drink and then return to the hotel to work on packing. It didn't quite work out that way," James confessed.

"Spill the beans – what happened?" I asked, more curious than mad.

"The police entered, looking for some drug dealers. No one was allowed to leave as they questioned each and every person in the pub," said Rodney.

"But you had your student ID's, showing that you were with an American university study abroad group. Didn't that help?"

"Actually, it hurt," commented Rodney, "because in their way of thinking, we would be leaving the country soon and out of harm's way."

"Why were they suspecting drugs in there in the first place?" I asked, curiously.

"There had been an anonymous phone call saying there would be a big drug deal last night in that particular pub," Brad explained.

"So they searched all of you who were in the pub?"

"Yes, and then took all of us to the police station to get fingerprints," said Lisa, who looked as though she hadn't slept in a week. "It was horrendous."

"This is crazy. They searched you and you didn't have anything. Why drag you to the police station for fingerprints?"

"Well, the police thought that perhaps the drug deal had already occurred, so the drugs were gone because they had been sold and the buyers had left. However, you would think if that were true, someone would have big bucks – or rather pounds since we're in England – on him.

"Had there been drug sales in there last night that you know of?" I asked.

"There had been some rough characters in there when we first went in, but they left fairly soon after we arrived. Maybe they had sold drugs to some of the customers who had also left," concluded James.

"Well, none of you were hurt. You were simply at the wrong place at the wrong time. If there's nothing more that you want to talk about concerning last night, I say that we put it behind us and move on. I'm just so glad that all of you are okay even though you lost a night's sleep."

They nodded.

"Is there anything else that you want to say about the whole experience?"

Everyone shook his head, too tired to think too much about the affair.

"Chalk it up to another adventure on our Study Abroad trip, and we move on. I want to tell you a little about Canterbury, but I think that I'll give you time to take an hour's nap and then enlighten you on Canterbury. What do you think?"

I got some winsome smiles, so I took that as a "yes," and I took out the last of the journals that I had to grade. I also brought along a book to read-up on Canterbury since it had been a while since I had visited the incredible city.

The students immediately got comfortable and closed their eyes to grab an hour's nap. I looked out the window from time to time to absorb the beautiful green, rolling hills of the southeastern part of England. Tiny white summer snowflakes and blue Jacob's ladder were prominent everywhere, and red poppies grew amass in some of the fields. Some of the plants were something called cotton grass. I didn't actually see the cotton grass growing, but the air was full of blowing cotton balls, and I knew that somewhere the cotton grass was hiding.

When I estimated that we were within half an hour from Canterbury, I timidly woke everyone.

"I'm so sorry to wake you, but I want to give you some information for your last journal, which will be due at breakfast time tomorrow morning. And then you are totally done doing your travel writing for this course," I said with a grin.

"I need to ask you if all of you have read Chaucer's *Canterbury Tales*?"

"Probably everyone has read it in high school," chimed in Lisa, "but it has been awhile."

"Okay, well, let me give you a little refresher course. During the late 14th century, Geoffrey Chaucer wrote a collection of twenty-four stories about pilgrims on their journey to Canterbury. It was likely a pilgrimage as many people traveled a long way to pay homage to Saint Thomas a Becket, who had been slain by four knights of Henry II on December 29, 1170. It was in Canterbury Cathedral where Becket's shrine was built.

"It was in Tabard Inn, a tavern in Southwark, a bit southwest of London, where the narrator of *The Canterbury Tales* began his story. The pilgrims, like the narrator, were traveling to the shrine of the martyred Saint Thomas a Becket. The Host of the story – whose name was Harry Bailey, and we found that out only in the Prologue to the Cook's Tale – suggested that the group ride together and entertain one another

THE FIRST PAGE OF THE KNIGHT'S TALE FROM
CHAUCER'S "THE CANTERBURY TALES"

with stories. Bailey decided that each pilgrim would tell two stories on the way to Canterbury and two on the way back. Bailey himself would judge who had told the best story, and that pilgrim would receive a meal at the tavern, courtesy of the other pilgrims."

"I certainly hope it wasn't the pub that we were in last night," James noted, jokingly.

"That's it," piped in Rodney. "The friar was there last night and had the drugs to sell. If I remember correctly, he was a bit sneaky and a money-hungry fellow in *The Canterbury Tales*."

That produced a chuckle from the class.

"Continue on, Professor Kira. It has been a while since some of us have read this," said Jessa.

"Well, Chaucer actually died before he finished *The Canterbury Tales*; nevertheless, we learned a great deal about the pilgrims from the stories that they told. Chaucer's hope was that readers would gather insights into customs and practices of the time period and gain an understanding of the various social classes. Even though the pilgrimage was based on a spiritual quest, it became obvious through the stories that some of the pilgrims were more concerned with worldly belongings than spiritual as Rodney has already pointed out. Although you probably didn't read all of *The Canterbury Tales* – the Knight, Squire, Monk, Friar, Cook, and Merchant are a few of the favorites – the entire works is perhaps his very best piece of literature and is often called Chaucer's magnum opus."

CHAPTER 14

I'LL BE ROAMIN' 'ROUND EUROPE

The train station was located at the edge of Westgate in Canterbury. We proceeded out of the train, and I rounded everyone up by the gate.

"I hope that you have your notebooks for the journals."

"We have been taking notes ever since you started talking about the cathedral on the train," chimed in Lisa.

"Awesome. I saw some of you taking notes, and you need to continue as there is so much information about Canterbury. Let's see...where to start? Oh, yes, this area has been inhabited since prehistoric times. We know this because archeologists have uncovered Paleolithic axes and Bronze Age pots. I want you to pay close attention to these historical structures," I commented, pointing first to an archaic wall. "This city wall was constructed during Roman times and then rebuilt or mended during the 14th century. Westgate was part of the Roman constructions.

"Also, of historical significance are the ruins of St. Augustine's Abby, a Norman castle, and the oldest, still existing school in the world. And speaking of schools, there are four universities here in Canterbury, so there is a substantial student population."

"Four universities are awesome in itself," said James. "And on top of all of this, they have the cathedral?"

"Yep, they do. Unfortunately, we don't have time to visit all these ancient structures except for the cathedral. We would need several days here to see it all.

"I've already told you many things about the cathedral but let me add just a little to those facts. After the murder of Saint Thomas a Becket at the cathedral in 1170, Canterbury became one of the most notable towns in all of Europe. Pilgrims from all parts of Christendom came to visit his shrine. All year long you could see thousands of pilgrims making their way on foot to Canterbury Cathedral. It really was and is such an important church and, as you'll soon see, incredibly amazing."

It took over half an hour's hike to get from Westgate to the cathedral. Once we rounded one of the corners of the main part of town, there it stood in all of its glory.

"Stop. I need a picture," said Jessa. "It's our first glimpse."

Everyone had to snap a picture. It was a glorious sight. Even so, we still had a twenty-minute walk before we were at the entrance of the cathedral.

"If I felt dwarfed by St. Paul's Cathedral, then I have to say that I feel like an ant here," commented

CANTERBURY CATHEDRAL

Rita. "How could we possibly find words to tell how we feel at this moment?"

"You're right, Rita. You really can't find words. I agree. Let me explain to you several details about the cathedral that I didn't tell you earlier. Much of the splendor that you're going to see is based on the wealth that the cathedral accrued from the pilgrimages. As money rolled in from the thousands of pilgrims each year, architects continued to add stained-glass windows, staircase towers, paintings, crypts, chandeliers, chapels, carvings, and many other features that are too numerous to name. I'm going to give you two hours to peruse the cathedral. You really need an entire day, but we still have to get back to London. Enjoy the treasures that you'll find in Canterbury Cathedral."

* * * *

We ended up spending three hours in the cathedral. The students couldn't get enough, and I was happy to give them an extra hour. I knew that it was an hour well spent. We ate a late, leisurely lunch in a café in Canterbury – The Duck Inn. Each of us ordered a different platter of food with the hopes of sharing and having a taste of various dishes of local cuisine. Knowing European standards, we wouldn't get our food for a good half hour, so I was people-watching until I overheard Sara and Katie talking about a bank box that didn't have a key, and my curiosity got the better of me.

"What are you girls talking about? Or is it something private?" I asked.

"Oh, no," answered Katie. "It's a hilarious story that my mom told me early last night when I called her." Everyone was listening by now.

"It seems that it happened to our neighbors – Elizabeth and Harry – who live next door. Elizabeth has Alzheimer's and knows very little most of the time.

"Anyway, Harry got a bank statement for twenty-five dollars for a safe deposit box in Elizabeth's name. The statement came as a surprise to Harry because he didn't know that his wife had a bank box. To top it off, neither did Elizabeth – not anymore because of her Alzheimer's. My mom loves drama so she says to me, 'What could be in the box, and more importantly, where could the key be?'"

Everyone was chuckling by now.

"Oh, my gosh," said Jessa, "so what happened?"

"Well, the bank would charge 500 dollars to open the box and then replace the lock and the keys. I guess that Harry says that he could afford to pay that; however, what if the box is empty or the contents are worthless? Then, too, maybe Elizabeth had been stashing money aside for some crazy reason and there were thousands in there." Katie stopped to laugh at the entire situation.

"Well, I told you it was a hilarious story, so nothing had been solved as of last night. My mom said, very dramatically, 'The question remains – what's in the box?'"

"You need to call her tonight to see if there's an update," chimed in Rodney. "She has everyone's curiosity peaked, and we need to know before we all disperse in Chicago."

"Well, you guys will just have to cling to me until I find my mom at the airport," concluded Katie, "because my mom will be gone all afternoon and well into the evening playing cards with her bridge club. I'd have to wait until 4:00 in the morning to reach her at 9:00 p.m. their time."

The story helped to pass the time until our platters arrived, and we enjoyed sharing our food, sampling the variety of delicacies that The Duck Inn had to offer.

By 4:00 we had finished our meal and stood at the gate to the train station. The train leaving for London was exactly on time – as are all trains in Europe – and we boarded, gearing up for the two-hour trip.

"I know that you're staying behind, Professor Kira, so will this be the last time that we're all together?" asked Katie.

"Oh, no, I'll take you to your plane tomorrow and see you off. You can't get rid of me yet," I said with a smirk.

"What will you do after we leave. You said that you'd be returning to Holland, and then where else?" Sara questioned.

"Yes, I'm going to catch a plane from London to Amsterdam. It departs an hour after you leave so that's perfect. I lived in the southeast part of Holland when I was there, and I've still got many friends there, so I'll take a train from Schiphol Airport in Amsterdam to Maastrict.

"I'm spending a week there, and then I'll take a train to Germany to visit cousins around the Munich area. We're having a reunion, so I'm sure to see all of my relatives. And the best part is that I have no journals or essays to grade although I have to say that all of you did an outstanding job on your written work. I'm very proud of you."

"All of us want to thank you for an incredible Study Abroad trip," commented Sara. "Indeed, we are all going back different people. We've grown and matured on this trip, and none of us saw that coming even after you told us we would."

"I'm the one who needs to be thanking you. I adore all of you guys, and I have loved watching you as you gained knowledge and viewed traditions of the old world," I said. "You know that I've always said that traveling through Europe is the best education that you can get. Education starts when you read about it, but the conclusion of understanding comes from travel. Experience is the real teacher. Thank you for the pleasure of leading you on that adventure."

As always when it came close to the time of departing, I'd tear up a bit because we had lived with each other for three weeks and had shared absolutely everything...well, almost everything. Tomorrow's departure would be even harder for me, and I always wished that I could suck it up and not be emotional.

"Well, don't worry, Professor Kira," commented James. "While we're getting readjusted to our boring lives back in the States and telling everyone of our amazing adventures, you'll still be jaunting through Europe, gathering more adventures to tell us when you return."

"Well, you guys do have plenty of great stories to

tell, though. Your mouths won't shut for a week," I said, laughing. "As for me, I'm hoping that I won't be experiencing another murder in my hotel or listening to a story of someone being mugged. Once was enough of those dreadful things. However, I chalk the trip up to a sensational time with stories that you can tell your children – well, at least, most of the stories are kid-friendly," I concluded.

"We need to stop at that outdoor café over there to have a wine and make a toast," commented Rita, pointing to tables, chairs, and umbrellas across the street.

"Let's do it," I answered.

We ordered wine, and I was about to comment on Canterbury when I saw everyone smiling. I looked around, trying to figure out what was funny when James handed me a small wrapped gift.

"We wanted to give you a little something so that you won't forget us," said James.

"Oh, you guys...."

I opened the package to find a brightly colored journal and a London pen.

"It's so you can journal on the rest of your trip – as we've been doing each day – and, hopefully, as you're doing that, you'll think of us," chimed in Rodney with a broad smile.

"And we've each written a short paragraph to relay to you how we have changed because of this trip. We truly don't want you to forget us because we won't forget you," commented Sara.

Tears were welling in my eyes again, and I decided

to just let them drip down my cheeks because there was no way to pretend they weren't there. I opened the book, and I saw that Sara had written the first passage.

I read, "Professor Kira discovered early-on my love of shopping. My favorite places were the open markets where I could meander and peruse the many priceless trinkets that were displayed. I believe that the ceramic mother duck with her three ducklings that I bought at Albert Cuypstraat market represents one thing that I'll take away from this trip. Just like the mother duckling who is leading her family through life, I have gained the responsibility of watching what is around me and learning from that so that I, too, can be a leader. Never was I as responsible as I am now. I'll look at life with an entirely different viewpoint and use my new, responsible nature to help me on the road to maturity."

Tears continued to drip, and I just let them fall.

"Here is what James said," I commented as I turned the page.

"This trip has opened my eyes to so many new ideas, but everyone will remember the one incident that changed me the most. I had longed for my bed to catch a few extra winks, and instead of sleep, I found disaster. I carried away not only emotional marks but also physical scars to assist me in not forgetting the situation. The moral of that story is that 'no man is an island,' and that staying within a group is not only comforting but also essential."

I read each and every person's paragraph with renewed love for that person, and I realized that truly they had all changed. I had one left to read, and it was Rodney's thoughts.

"I have to thank Professor Kira for the numerous lessons in history that she gave me. I had the opportunity to see incredible churches that are beyond physical description to someone who has never seen them. I got to see buildings and monuments that I had only read about in textbooks. I even had the chance to ride in different modes of transportation – ferry, chunnel, canal boats, bikes as well as bike taxis, and trams. The one piece of history that amazed me the most, though, was the Red Light district of Amsterdam."

Everyone let out a howl now as we hadn't really expected that.

"I got to personally see the oldest profession in the world in action – well, sort of – and I got to see it not once but twice. Viewing everything from the canal boat was great as we saw the scene bathed in red neon lights! I just want to thank Professor Kira for offering us the chance of roamin' 'round Europe. It was an incredible trip for all of us."

"Well, let's make a toast then," chimed in Sara, "for this incredible trip that has changed each and every one of us and to our friendship that I hope never ends."

"I, too, change every time that I take a group of students to Europe," I comment. "I grow as a person the same as you do. I learn through all of you young people. So here's to roamin' 'round Europe!"

ACKNOWLEDGMENTS

I'd like to thank my best friend (and also an English instructor), Christy Wolfer Loy. She's the person to whom I go when it comes to editing. After I've edited multiple times, I send it along to Chris who always finds mistakes that I overlook. Thank you, dear friend.

ABOUT THE AUTHOR

THE AUTHOR ROAMIN' 'ROUND
THE NETHERLANDS

J AN FRAZIER has been in the field of education for over forty years – first in secondary schools and most recently at the university level. Having retired in the spring of 2020, she has plans on doing more traveling. Taking students to Europe on study-abroad trips was always a joy, and she felt that she learned as much as the students did on such trips because she got to see Europe through the eyes of the students. Jan believed that only so much could be taught within the four walls of the classroom, and then the students needed to get into the world to "see" for themselves.

Jan has been honored with various awards for teaching as well as for her writing abilities. She has twenty-one books to her credit.

WORKS CITED

Canterbury Cathedral. Official Cathedral Publication. London: 1995. Print.

Luciano, Phil. *Pekin Daily Times*. Pekin: 2020. Print.

Pascoe, Robin and Christopher Catling. *Eyewitness Travel Guide Amsterdam*. A Dorling Kindersley Book. New York: 1995. Print.

Porter, Darwin and Danforth Prince. *Frommer's London*. MacMillan Publishing Company. New York : 1997. Print.

Tillier, Alan. *Eyewitness Travel Guide Paris*. A Dorling Kindersley Book. New York: 1997. Print.

www.hellgatepress.com

www.ingramcontent.com/pod-product-compliance
Lightning Source LLC
Chambersburg PA
CBHW071359170626
46811CB00003B/1187

* 9 7 8 1 5 5 5 7 1 9 8 9 0 *